BODIES AND SHADOWS

BY PETER WEISS

BODIES

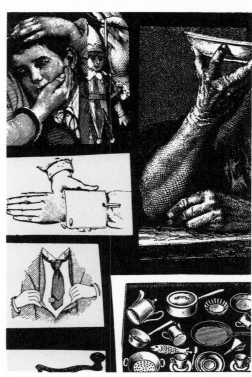

A SEYMOUR LAWRENCE BOOK
DELACORTE PRESS / NEW YORK

AND SHADOWS

TWO SHORT NOVELS BY **PETER WEISS**

TRANSLATORS
E. B. Garside/Rosemarie Waldrop

Originally published in Germany
by Suhrkamp Verlag, Frankfurt am Main,
in two volumes under the titles
Das Gesprach der drei Gehenden and
Der Schatten des Körpers des Kutschers.

Library of Congress Catalog Number: 70-90906
Manufactured in the United States of America
First Printing

DESIGNED BY *Larry Kamp*

CONTENTS

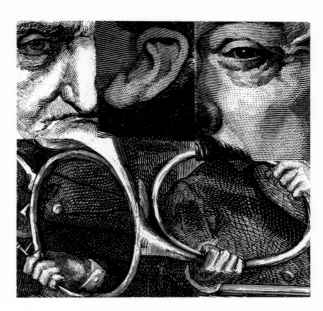

THE SHADOW OF
THE COACHMAN'S BODY

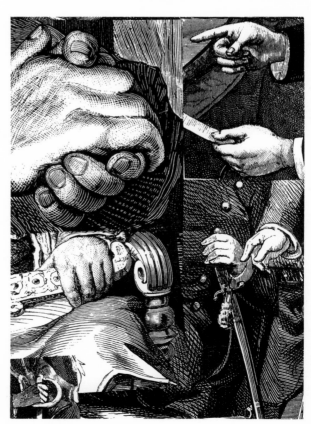

TRANSLATED FROM THE GERMAN BY

E. B. Garside

THROUGH the half-open door I see the muddy, trampled path and the rotten planks around the pigsty. The snout of the pig sniffs along the wide crevice whenever it isn't rooting in the mud, snorting and grunting. Besides this I also see part of the house, its wall with the yellowish plaster cracked and partly crumbling off, a few posts with horizontal pegs for the clothes lines, and farther back, as far as the horizon, moist black soil. These are the sounds: the smacking and grunting of the pig's snout, the slopping and splattering of the mud, the bristly rubbing of the pig's back against the planks, the squeaking and cracking of the planks, the rattling of the planks and loose posts at the wall of the house, the occasional soft whistling of the wind at the corner of the house and the gusts of wind sweeping over the furrows, the croaking of a crow far away which hasn't been repeated yet (it cried harm), the soft creaking and crackling in the wood of the little house where I sit, the dripping of the last of the rain from the tar-paper roof, hollow and hard when a drop hits a stone or the ground, plinking when a drop hits a puddle, and the rasping of a saw, from the shed. The jerky back-and-forth of the saw, now stopping for a moment, now violently starting up again, indicates that it is in the hand of the hired man. Even without this special characteristic, often heard and confirmed and verified, I would not find it hard to guess that the hired man is handling the saw. Aside from him, only I

take care of the wood in the shed, and on rare occasions
the captain but only early in the morning and with unmistakable slowness; unless of course a new boarder has just
arrived and, wishing to recover from the stiffness in his
bones after the long coach trip, might be using the saw,
bending forward and drawing backward with a taut back
and thrusting and pulling with his arm. But I haven't heard
the coach come in, neither the clopping of the wheels and
straps, nor the rumble of the body, neither the horn signal
that the coachman usually gives on arriving nor the tongue
clicking nor the drumming sound he makes with his
tongue to tell the horse to stop. Nor have I heard the
stamping of the horse, and on the wet dirt road I certainly
would have been able to hear it. And if the boarder had
arrived on foot it is unlikely that he would go straight to
the shed, and even if he had stepped into the shed, maybe
from curiosity, his tiredness after the long hike (a day's
walk from the nearest town) and the thick and shapeless
pieces of root and trunk would have kept him from work.
I insist then that it is the hired man who, in the shed, thrusts
the saw into the heavy logs and pulls it back and forth; I
see him in front of me in his shirt that was once blue but
has long faded and is crusty with dirt and his equally
crusty, once black, pants which he has tucked into the
legs of his clumsy boots, also black once but plastered with
dung and mud. I see him in front of me holding the piece
of wood on the jack with one earthy, thick-veined, short-
fingered hand while spanning the handle of the saw with
the other, pushing his long lower lip over his short upper
lip and licking off the slime trickling from his nose; I hear
him humming from his throat, cooing as he does when
working in the house or outside; and in the short, irregular
stops between the sawing I can imagine him straightening
his back, and bending far backward and stretching his arms
out on both sides and cracking his knuckles, or blowing

his nose with his thumb and index finger and then wiping it with the back of his hand, or pushing his greasy cap with ear flaps turned up off of his forehead far back on his head and softly scratching his thin, sticky strands of hair creased by the sweat band of his cap. Only now (the crow is just crying harm again) I feel cold on my bare seat. Writing down my observations has kept me from pulling my pants up and buttoning them; or the sudden start of my observations made me forget to pull up my pants; or maybe it was the lowered pants, the shivering, the concentration coming over me here in the outhouse that brought about this particular mood for observation. I now pull up my pants, button them and buckle the belt; I take the wooden lid, but before putting it on the opening I look down into the bucket filled to the brim with the brownish mass of excrement and paper with brown stains; as far as I can tell in the darkness of the box, the feces have even overflowed the rim of the bucket; the thick stream ends in a lava-like mound in which the bucket is half buried; the brightness of the shreds of paper gleams out of the black. After putting the lid on I sit down again on the box, the writing pad on my knees. The inside walls of the outhouse are covered with grainy tar paper; however, the moisture has made the paper bulge with enormous boils, and in some places it is torn and hanging down in tatters; the thin, moldy gray slats are bare underneath. A few rusty nails stick out of the wall, perhaps meant to hang clothes on or some utensils, but now empty and bent; not even a piece of string, a wire or a bundle of paper is hanging there. As for paper, everyone rips as much as he needs from the torn-up newspapers stacked at the corner of the seat. Now and then, after much reminding, the hired man brings these newspapers from the basement where they lie in a heap beside the coal, crumpled and dusty, having been used as wrapping around some delivered merchandise or left by travelers and read again and again, greasy, worn out, often put to further use in the kitchen, full of black skillet rims and imprints of plates and cups, with potato peels and fish bones sticking to them. And here, in the outhouse, these remains of newspapers with most of their information many years old, find another reader; sitting bent forward, one's feet propped on the ledge in front of the box, one gets absorbed in small, mixed-up fragments of time, in events without beginning or end, often even divided crosswise or up and down; one follows one person's speech and continues with the speech of another, one reads the description of the scene of an action and then glides on to the scene of a different action, one learns something which is denied in the next piece and yet proven to exist again in the one following that; one finds similar events furnished again and again with new details, or even comes across the same, here fitted with certain archaisms and there with some innovation. I shove my left foot forward, prop my writing arm on my right leg and push the door a bit further open. I now see the entire back wall of the house rising high and bare over the pigsty, with pointed gable and a roof which comes out far beyond the side walls, and one of the side walls, foreshortened, with the stone steps to the kitchen door, the stairs to the basement, and the narrow recesses of the windows, one of which, the window of the family's room, is open; a few pieces of cloth, probably diapers, are spread out on the sill. The ground around the house is, like the road and the fields, muddy and full of puddles; here and there are stones, large and small, some loose rubble, some sticking out of the ground with a whitish curve or edge, some heaped into small pyramids, some arranged in rows according to form and size; next to one of the heaps, a crowbar and a shovel are sticking in the ground. On the smooth handles of these tools I can imagine Mr. Schnee's hands, unusually large, bony hands with fingernails arched like shields; his work accumulates dirt under their long edges which right after work, however, is carefully removed with a silver nail file which Mr. Schnee keeps in the pocket of his vest. The stones too have gone through Mr. Schnee's hands, they have been felt, turned, and rolled over in his fingers; we can assume that he is now standing at the window of his room and looking down at the yard, waiting for the sun to dry the heaps of stones. In the course of time, he has dug up and examined large quantities of stones; many stones which he considered unsuitable he has carted in a wheelbarrow to a heap behind the woodshed, other stones which he plans to study he has carried up to his room where he keeps them on shelves all around the walls.

I am now in my room since the outhouse had to be used by another boarder whom we call the tailor because he sews his own clothes from old rags. The tailor appeared on the kitchen steps and walked toward the outhouse, in slippers, tiptoeing cautiously around the puddles, his head lowered, a pipe in his mouth. I cleared my throat and he was startled. He was terribly upset, a state he always gets into when meeting one of the other boarders unexpectedly; the pipe dropped out of his mouth, and while he bent down and fumbled for it, his glasses, held together by a thin wire, slid from his nose. His hands were burrowing in the yellowy mud water; I helped him, handed him the glasses and the pipe, and for a while he tried to put the glasses as a pipe into his mouth and the pipe as glasses to his eyes until finally the things found their proper places; drops of wet mud ran down his face. He wanted to turn and go back, but he was stuck; his hands alternately flapping up and down and wrung together; he was still standing that way after I had left him and was walking along the path

7

toward the kitchen steps. Looking up to the house I saw, as I had suspected, Mr. Schnee standing at his window; his big, pale face to the pane, like a fish with his flattened nose, his broad, pouting lips licking the glass, and the bulging, colorless eyes. Walking by the open window on the ground floor, I had a short look into the family's room. I noticed the father, the mother, the infant, and the son in the following distribution and relation to each other: the mother sitting on the edge of the bed at the back of the room, half in the dark, her breast bared, and the infant at her breast; the father standing at the table in the middle of the room, his fists propped on the tabletop in front of him, the light from the window full on him, outlining the face thrust forward with the mouth wide open; and opposite him, not sitting but squatting on his heels, the son, his chin pressed against the edge of the table, his shoulders pulled up to the ears, staring into the father's open mouth. Then I reached the stairs, and this is the way I went to my room: I opened the kitchen door and closed it behind me; I went across the worn gray linoleum of the kitchen which was moist from being scrubbed, and where the housekeeper was on her knees and elbows, the scouring cloth in her hand, looking up at me in silence as I passed, with her thin dress wet at the loins and arms and tightly clinging to the heavy curves of her body. My next goal was the threshold of the opening to the hall; this I approached while the objects in the kitchen were gliding by: at my right, the stove with the flue of white-painted brick above it, a pot of potatoes, a second pot full of carrots bubbling on the fire, next to the stove the sink at the wall, filled with plates and cups, and the table, below the window, dusted with flour, with rolled dough on a board and a few big kneaded lumps of dough, a wooden rolling pin, a bowl of sugar and a spoon, and at each long side of the table a slim bench stained dark as well as a stool at each of the narrow sides of the table; to my left the huge cupboard, its doors and drawers shut, next to it the grandfather clock of brown wood, under its glass the pendulum ticking slowly back and forth in front of the weights in the shape of fir cones. After having reached the threshold I had my next goal in front of me, the stairs rising narrow and steep from the hall; there is some dim light from an overhead window; its bluish shimmer, aided by the pale light from the kitchen, barely lights the space. I grazed the edge of the sewing machine which had faint silver reflections on its spools and metal parts, went by the round table in whose open drawer I more assumed than saw buttons, hooks, needles and thread, and hit the silk lampshade above it with my shoulder; it swayed back and forth with softly fluttering tassels. Then I passed Schnee's armchair letting my hand glide over the wooden arm rest and the straight, high back with its round tacks in the leather; back to back with this armchair is the captain's armchair on three legs; instead of the fourth, a couple of bricks support it; both the seat and the back have split open and show the plaited cords and the springs; above the back which is decorated with a wooden knob (of the other missing knobs only the peg holes bear witness) there hung some straps and a belt with a scabbard. Next to the empty umbrella stand and the empty coat hooks I could make out the front door of the house in the half dark, but I took my eyes off it now that I had reached the stairs. I put my hands on the banisters and climbed step after step on the reddish rug which is fastened down with brass rods; my hands pulled me and my feet under which the steps were creaking pushed me higher and higher; above, I saw the landing which turns into the hall of the second floor. I reached the landing with a last pull of my arms while my hands held on to the top knobs on the banisters. Before being able to climb the stairs up to the attic I had to traverse the length of the hall. On both sides of the hall there are, one beside the other, the doors to the rooms of the hired man, the housekeeper, the captain, the doctor, Mr. Schnee and the tailor, brown doors with brass handles and keyholes; and up high, in the lightshaft over the stairs, one can see the bluish glass of the garret window. The narrow rug runs from the stairs through the hall; its black edges look like rails, and walking along I seemed to be rolling in a car to the attic stairs. Here, I again put my hands on the banisters and climbed to the last but one goal, the attic. Up there I saw my last goal in front of me, the door to my room; and I went toward this door under the rafters, past the high square beams that carry the weight of the roof, past the boxes, baskets and suitcases that are stored under the rafters, past the chimney until I could reach the door handle with my hand; but this moment is long past, the moment of opening the door, of entering, of receiving the image of the room, of closing the door, of the way to the table; past also is the time that has gone by with the description of my way here. I am now lying stretched out on my bed.

Besides the daily operations of dressing and undressing, washing, going to bed and getting up, and the attempts at writing which have never yet gone beyond always new, short, broken-off beginnings, my activity in this room is to bring up images. For this, I lie stretched out on the bed; within reach, beside me, on the table, there is a plate full of salt from which I occasionally take a few grains to put in my eyes. The function of the salt is to stimulate the tear glands and thus blur my vision; the resulting tear threads, light points, and swelling or dissolving wedges of light are superimposed on the image of the room which is clearly etched into my retina; and even though this room contains nothing but a table, a chair, a washstand, a bed, and even though there is nothing on the sloping wall but the window above the table, and only a door in the opposite, straight wall, and nothing on the two other walls which are cut by the roof, even so my look is still trapped by these limits and fixed forms; with my tears I dissolve them. While I look straight ahead with wide-open eyes, the uncertain, flickering shadows, beams, prisms, splotches of color, and lines gradually gather into the first suggestions of figures, interrupted, in the beginning, by sudden tinges of total black. The results of these experiments on which I've spent hardly more than ten minutes, at most a quarter of an hour, are as follows: first, I discerned a curve, like a balloon or a glass ball of indefinite color, sometimes tending toward green, sometimes toward yellow or blue, and growing more and more luminous and intense. This ball could be a lamp or simply some big decoration hanging down into a room; around the ball, colored ribbons of shiny silk or thin metal joined, and the ball grew upward with new curves, swellings, grooves like those that grow out of clay on the wheel, in the hands of the potter. The shape radiated in the colors of the rainbow against a black background from which new details now came forward. Dappled planes in purple and pink suggested depth; however, one could not see the space as a whole; it seemed to dissolve into the infinite. From the background, which was constantly shifting and sometimes showed a moving marbled wall or a piece of a polished floor, emerged single smaller balls, these too shimmering in a glassy fire, and figures like castles from a game of chess or ballet dancers; they were of the same material as the balls, but their shape more ephemeral; while the balls were stretching and expanding, the figures changed without pause, they resembled plants, minerals, sculptures, crystals, or simply rose as undefinable beings from the dark, a mere play of colors and shapes. Holding my breath I followed their movements until suddenly, after I had felt the picture fading and put a few more grains of salt in my eyes, the scene changed. Now it was as though I were leaning against the railing of a balcony, high over a city at night; the indefinable space of the former image gave way to the distinct hugeness of a celestial dome. Deep down there was a street with roofs spread out around it, but the street was no more than a black ravine, or just a narrow crack; and directly below me, on the roof garden of the house opposite, there gleamed a face as if in moonlight, yet there was no moon nor any stars, a face with thin cheekbones, a full, dark mouth, dark shaded eyes, and under the face a slim throat against the flowing hair, and under the edge of the throat the sharply outlined collar bone with the bare straight shoulders, and under the shoulders the bare breasts circumscribed by lines of shadows, with the black centers of the nipples, and under the breasts the ribs suggested by dim shadows and the smooth bare round of the belly with the dark center of the navel, and under the belly the triangular dark of the womb and the slim angular hips, and under the hips, down to the cut-off line of the stone parapet, the long curves of the thighs; I bent over the railing toward the female body; I felt her nearness so strongly that I took the mirage for reality and made a hasty movement with my arms which immediately tore the image.

We eat supper, like all other meals, at the kitchen table. In spite of the wealth of dishes in the cupboard, the table is set with a minimum of plates, cups, bowls, and silverware, so that a possible appetizer and a possible dessert are eaten on the same plate as the main course, a deep plate of white china. For eating tools, each uses only one tin spoon for all the courses as well as for stirring in the mug from which he drinks his water, beer, wine or coffee. Not much store is set on the cleanliness of the tabletop, in contrast to the floor which is scrubbed several times daily by the housekeeper; thus the table is still full of flour and lumps of dough, and of dried breadcrumbs and gristle from former meals. This is the order in which the boarders are sitting around the table: on the stool at the upper narrow side of the table, next to the stove, the housekeeper; to her left, on the bench in front of the wall with the window, the captain in a black old-fashioned cutaway with white stripes, like pants, a gray vest which, in spite of his pains-taking care, has not escaped a few spots in the course of the years, a white shirt with a high stand-up collar, and a black tie fastened with a pearl clasp; to the left of the captain, Mr. Schnee, who in the evening is wrapped in his silk house coat; to the left of Mr. Schnee, the doctor with thickly bandaged head, a band-aid across his nose and a band-aid on his upper lip, a bandage around his neck, bandages around his wrists, enormously thick bandages on his legs, his mouth shut tight over the pain that seems to fill his whole body and threatens to break from his mouth, his eyes hidden behind black glasses. At the other narrow side of the table, the hired man is sitting with his cap on his head; to his left, at the other long side of the table, the tailor in his threadbare pieced-together suit, piebald as a harlequin, describing, since he has prepared himself for this meeting, large curves, capricious arabesques, and wild angles with gestures so calculated that they constantly outgrow themselves. To the left of the tailor, I am sitting. To my left, nobody; the place is empty and waiting for a new boarder. (The family who live in the room next to the kitchen do not take part in our meals; they keep house for themselves.) In the middle of the table are the two pots, one filled with potatoes, the other with carrots. Hands holding spoons are now lifted toward the pots from all sides; the house-keeper's hand red, swollen, dishwaterlogged; the captain's hand with polished, grooved fingernails; the doctor's hand with bandage slings between all fingers; the hired man's hand spotty with dung and mud; the tailor's hand trembling, skinny, like parchment; my own hand, my own hand; and then no hand, in an empty space waiting for a hand. The spoons dip into the pots and come out laden with potatoes and carrots, discharge their load onto the plates and swing back to the pots, fill up, unload over the plates, continue to wander back and forth until each has assembled on his plate a heap of potatoes and carrots according to his appetite. The biggest heap is on the hired man's plate, but the heap on the tailor's plate is nearly as big although the tailor doesn't, like the hired man, spend most of his day outside in strenuous physical labor, but only sits in his room over his rags; next, the heap on the housekeeper's plate, barely distinguishable (and only after several precise comparisons) from the heap on Schnee's plate; then the captain's heap which is already small compared with the heap on the hired man's plate; then the heap on my own plate which can be called little, but still seems big in relation to the heap on the doctor's plate. Now the spoons full of pieces of potatoes and carrots rise to the mouths; the mouths open: the housekeeper's mouth as if for a sucking kiss while she wheezingly blows through her nose; the captain's mouth cautiously maneuvering his false teeth; Schnee's mouth with the broad lips pulled back, bared and whitish; the doctor's mouth splitting in a painful crevice; the hired man's mouth pushed forward like a beak, the tongue sticking way out expecting the spoon; the tailor's mouth popping open foppishly and widening to lockjaw; my own mouth, my own mouth; and then the empty space for a new, still unknown mouth. Thus we chew our first bite: the housekeeper slowly, circular, grinding; the captain gnashing his false teeth; Schnee smacking his lips and bending over his plate; the doctor gulping without moving his teeth, mashing his food with his tongue against his palate; the hired man slurping, his arms heavy on the table; the tailor leering at the hired man's plate, his jaw muscles trembling and sticking out like cords, his tongue licking the spittle-soaked pap; I, I; and then the one whose chewing I don't know about. This is the way we eat, silently; the hired man, the tailor, and the housekeeper load their plates another time; they, however, catch up with the other eaters so that we all finish about the same time. Between movements of the spoons, the tin mugs are occasionally grabbed by the other hands; the housekeeper's mug is filled with beer; the captain's mug is filled with water; Schnee's mug is filled with dark red wine which he poured from a bottle kept in the pocket of his house coat; the doctor's mug contains a few drops of water; the hired man's mug is filled with beer; the tailor's mug is filled with water, as is my own, and what would the unknown boarder fill his mug with. The mugs are lifted to the mouths and the liquid penetrates into the mouths, fills the mouths except with the doctor who only moistens the split in his mouth, thin as a notch from a knife. While the hand's grip on the spoon is nearly the same with all, each distinguished rather by his way of raising his hand: with the house-keeper, arm and hand keep a nearly fixed position and it is the upper part of her body that goes up and down; the captain makes a cracking lever movement with his elbow; Schnee's hand moves the spoon from the wrist back and forth between the plate and his lowered mouth; the hired man's hand pushes the spoon like a coal shovel into his mouth gaping like a furnace door in front of the plate; the tailor's arm jerks and jumps like a wound-up doll; I, I hardly notice how I eat for watching the others—the grip on the mug is strongly characteristic with each: the house-keeper takes the mug with a rounded hand, she slides her hand under the mug and lifts it in her hand as in a bowl toward the mouth; the captain puts the tips of his crooked fingers on the mug, holds the mug as in the tongs of a bird's claw; Schnee feels the mug with his long bone-white fingers, and while he lifts the mug his fingers seem to milk it; the doctor presses the mug between his free hand and the hand that holds the spoon, and, in a concerted effort, both hands clamp the mug to the mouth; the hired man puts his hand around the mug like a mound of earth and tips the mug into the approaching mouth; the tailor who, when not drinking, keeps his flat hand as a lid on the mug, flips his hand sideways for drinking, then snaps his thumb down and his fingers around and moves the mug as in a box; I myself feel the cool roundness of tin in the inside of my hand. The following incidents happened during the meal: at the beginning, when we had hardly taken our seats, one could hear the cawing of the crow from the fields; it was a single cry sounding like harm as before. When our spoons began scraping the full plates we heard through the wall also the clatter of dishes on the family's table; the infant blubbered, but calmed down soon, probably being given suck; a sound like a tin spoon hitting a tin mug and then a few seconds complete silence behind the wall were followed by another noise, like a belt coming down hard on a body, repeated several times until there was silence again; soon after, the usual clanking of dishes continued. A coughing fit of the tailor's was, beside the doctor's one smothered groan, the only interruption of the monotony of our meal; the only other thing to be noted is the appearing and disappearing of a black medium-sized bug; it fell from the flue onto the top of the stove, was lucky enough to land on its legs (if it had fallen on its back the heat of the stove would have charred it) and quickly ran to the edge of the stove from where it looked down into the sink. Its forelegs felt for the start of the sink, the body followed, and that way he slid down; I stood up

and saw it disappear into one of the holes of the strainer.
Which death, I asked myself, is easier for a beetle, or less
painful, death by burning on a stove or death by drowning
in a drainpipe. We drink our coffee in the hall after the
plates, stacked by the boarders, have been carried to the
sink by the housekeeper, and the mugs, filled from the blue
pot by the housekeeper, have been carried through the
kitchen by the boarders, and the boarders have taken a
piece of sugar from the sugarbowl the housekeeper has
brought from the larder, put it in the cup, and have crossed
the threshold and sat down in the hall stirring in their
mugs with spoons which all but the doctor have licked
clean: the housekeeper on the chair in front of the sewing
machine, the captain on his armchair supported by bricks,
back to back with the armchair where Mr. Schnee has sat
down, the doctor on the umbrella stand, the hired man on
a folding chair he had pulled from under the stairs, the
tailor completely in the shadow on the floor near the front
door, and myself on the third step of the stairs. Hardly has
everyone found his place and put the edge of the mug to
his lips and felt the black, hot coffee run to the tip of his
tongue, when the door to the family's room opens and the
father comes out, also holding a tin mug, which he is stirring
with a tin spoon, and after him the mother, with the same
kind of mug and spoon, and after the mother the son,
carrying a chair in each hand. He puts the chairs down between the housekeeper's chair and the armchairs of the
captain and Mr. Schnee and pushes them under the father
and mother who sit down on the chairs; then he turns and
goes back into the room and shuts the door behind him.
The monotony of the common meal in the kitchen grows
here, in the hall, into a diversity of occurrences. The mere
irregular distribution of boarders in the room makes right
away for a pattern of interconnected movements and
sounds that is hard to survey. The housekeeper puts her

17

mug on the sewing machine and reaches into the drawer of the sewing table where the buttons rattle in her fingers; the tailor scrapingly pulls up his legs and crosses them, then he takes his pipe from his hip pocket and begins stuffing it with tobacco which he has pulled out of his side pocket; the captain too reaches into a pocket, his vest pocket, takes out a silver case, knocks on the lid, snaps the lid open, leans over the back of the armchair, hands the case over Schnee's shoulder; Schnee turns toward him, thrusts his hand with a wide curve into the case, lifts a cigarette out of it whereupon the captain takes the case back, takes a cigarette out of the case himself, snaps the case shut and puts it back into his vest pocket. Then the captain reaches into his pants pocket and makes his hand come out with a lighter; the hand with the lighter swings over the back of the armchair, Schnee turns his face toward the lighter, the captain's fingers strike fire, and Schnee sucks at the flame with the cigarette in his mouth. The face of the captain turned over the back is close to Schnee's face, the eyes of both of them look sideways at the lighter, and the flame is reflected in their pupils; after the tip of Schnee's cigarette starts glowing and he blows a cloud of blue smoke from his lips, the captain puts the flame to his own cigarette, and Schnee watches him sucking on the cigarette, and this cigarette too starting to glow, and the smoke flowing from the captain's mouth. The father leans forward and takes the scabbard which has been hanging on the back of the armchair since the afternoon when the captain probably busied himself with it; he lifts it up to himself and fingers it; the captain turns to him, takes hold of the belt fastened to the scabbard, pushes the scabbard farther toward the father, but without letting go of the belt. While they are exchanging words which I cannot hear because of the distance and their talking softly, the captain leans still more toward the father, the belt in his hand, the father runs his finger along the scabbard up to the belt and puts his index finger into the sheath. Schnee too turns toward the scabbard and of the words which he contributes to the conversation I distinguish: rust and clean. Meanwhile the mother has moved closer to the housekeeper, and between her and the housekeeper there are also words exchanged of which I understand a few, like pap, threading, airing, the boy, take care of the baby, wash dishes later, for Sunday, give food, give suck, hurt, pinches so. The housekeeper has pulled a linen shirt from the lower drawer of the table and starts sewing a button where the collar begins; Schnee takes a few small stones from one pocket of his house coat (the neck of the bottle is sticking out of the other), weighs them in his hand and holds them over the scabbard, under the eyes of the captain and the father; the lines of vision gather with Schnee's own into a bundle on the stones; I hear some of the words from the series of statements that Schnee pronounces: for instance, especially, dried out, streaked, just two more, will try tomorrow, sometime deeper, from that point, still not, after all, if one sometime, might be. The father reaches with the hand he had put into the sheath for the stones and fingers them, and among his words I discern: have of course, maybe work, just hangs around, good for nothing, will ask him right away. At that he turns toward the door to the family's room and whistles between his teeth; from the room we can hear a crash as if a chair were falling over, the door is thrown open, and the son appears, runs over the threshold with hunched shoulders, leaves the door open behind him, runs through the hall past the chairs of the mother and the housekeeper, runs, bumping into the lamp which sways back and forth with fluttering tassels, to the father's chair. The father lifts his hand and hooks his index finger into the uppermost buttonhole of the son's jacket while keeping hold of his mug with his thumb, middle finger, ring finger and little finger, and pulls the son's torso down to his ear. In the family's room which is lit by a bulb hanging from the ceiling, I can see the infant lying on the green cover of the bed, his legs in the air, groping with his hands for his feet, sometimes getting hold of a toe and losing it again, straining to raise his head and letting it fall back again. From the conversation into which the son is drawn I get the following: words of the father's like early, usefulness, Mr. Schnee's activity, looked on long enough, show for once, barrow, shovel, sand, seven, eight, nine stones, cart away, clean, line up; words said by Mr. Schnee like of course, be cautious, careful, understand what about, three thousand seven hundred seventy-two stones to date, learn from the beginning, count on remuneration too; interjected words of the captain's like better, very well, not the worst, in my time, much changed. During the negotiations, the son is not looking at the father and not at Mr. Schnee or the stones in front of him, but across at me; his hair hangs into his knitted brows, his lips rub against his teeth, and his skin twitches around his deepset, black eyes staring out of the white. The mother whose face had been lowered over the housekeeper's work, straightens up now and leans over sideways with her hand stretched out to the son; she pulls at the hem of his jacket; Schnee snaps the long nail of his index finger against one of the stones; the captain pulls the scabbard back to himself; it slides slowly through the father's hand; the mother tugs at the hem of the son's jacket; the jacket is raised by the son's shoulders; through the mother's pulling the jacket slides down along with the sinking shoulders of the son, until the hem of the jacket is hanging over his knees like a skirt and his shoulders have subsided to a tilted plane. The captain has pulled the scabbard from the father's hand, he raises the scabbard and lightly touches the son's hanging shoulder with it while the mother is still holding on to the hem of the son's jacket and the father's index finger is still hooked in the buttonhole of the jacket. From the dark under the stairs there are sounds that indicate a change in the situation, and I see now that the tailor has, probably on all fours, come up to the hired man, and probably because the hired man waved to him with a pack of cards. The hired man's hand deals the cards with flapping smacks on the floor so that a heap grows in front of him and another in front of the tailor. Then they arrange the cards in their hands, whereupon the hired man, bending far down from his folding chair, pulls out a card and throws it heavily on the floor, and the tailor, sitting with his legs crossed, makes the same gesture, only more elaborately. In this manner things go back and forth between them; and behind them, leaning his back against the umbrella stand, I can see the doctor, his face distorted with pain, one hand unwrapping the bandage from the wrist of the other. Between card throws, the hired man and the tailor now and then take a sip from the mugs they have put on the floor beside them; the captain and Mr. Schnee too occasionally take a sip from the mugs which Schnee is balancing on one of his knees and the captain has clamped between his two knees. The father also takes a sip from the mug pulling the son's chest down with his hooked finger, and also the mother, who has turned away from the son again, drinks from the mug she has placed on the sewing machine beside the housekeeper's mug; and also the housekeeper now and then interrupts her work and slurps a mouthful; and I also take a gulp from the mug whose warm roundness lies between my hands. The loose parts of the bandage at the doctor's wrist have blood and pus stains; he continues to unwrap while rolling up the loose part; and the house-keeper's hand with needle and thread glides up and down; and the mother tilts her head back and yawns with wide-open mouth; and the father's index finger lets go of the buttonhole in the son's jacket; and Schnee's hand with the stones sinks back into the pocket of the house coat; and the captain lifts the tails of his cutaway and buckles the belt with the scabbard; and the doctor, with contorted mouth, tears the last bit of bandage from his wrist and looks at the flaming red skin laid bare; and the captain and Mr. Schnee lean their heads back so that the backs of their heads touch; and the tailor, the first round of the game done, is now shuffling the cards; and the son tiptoes off backward toward the open door to the family's room; and the housekeeper's teeth bite off the thread; and the mother scratches under her breasts; and the doctor leaves his place and comes toward the stairs holding the inflamed wrist in his other hand; and the tailor deals the cards; and the housekeeper rummages among the buttons in the drawer and pulls out a new button which she holds against the front of the shirt; and the son reaches, walking backward, the threshold, steps over the threshold, and pulls the door shut in front of him, going backward into the room; and the doctor walks past me up the creaking steps; I move to the side; I hear him groaning softly; in the baggy pocket of his jacket his mug of coffee sploshing.

After everybody had retired to his room, except for the housekeeper who went to the kitchen to wash the floor, and after even the housekeeper, the job finished, had turned out the light in the kitchen, the hall, and the stairwell, and shut the door of her room behind her, I heard again, lying on my bed, the noise, the shuffling, hitting and screaming downstairs. Since this noise was familiar from other evenings I knew that it came from the family's room, and although the course of the disturbance was known I asked myself again, as always, whether I should go down to help, or interfere, or just stand in front of the door and wait.

And as always, I remained lying down for a while thinking that the noise would stop by itself although I knew it would not stop by itself; I put a few grains of salt in my eyes, but no pictures came; I only heard the noise rise up the stairs in muted waves. Then I got up, I had already taken off my shoes, and went in stocking feet down the dark stairs. I stopped in front of the door of the family's room, and from behind the door I heard the cracking voice of the father, the blubbering of the infant, the sobbing of the mother, the panting breath of the son. My eyes gradually got used to the dark; high above the stairs I noticed the pale purple-blue square of the garret window; and the black of the hall was not so dark that I couldn't see the furniture as still darker shades of black. I bent down to the keyhole and peered into the room where the mother was sitting on the edge of the bed pressing the infant to her, and the father was running after the son around a chair which the son was holding in front of himself; the father had grabbed the hem of the son's jacket; the jacket was stretched taut, and the chest of the son pulling forward; and the father screamed words of which I got the following: will you, across my knee, what I, if you won't, will you, I tell you, that you, I'll; between these words there was a bubbling of words in which his tongue got tangled. Sobbing and rocking the infant in front of her breasts, the mother screamed words at the son each time he ran past her; and of her words which were partly drowned in the sobs and partly interrupted by the humming sounds with which she tried to calm the infant, I caught these: that you, how can you, it'll get, now lie down, deserved, otherwise you'll, now stop, you have to, now stand still, you'll make him, he'll get, he has to. All of a sudden, the son stopped so abruptly that the father bumped into him, nearly knocked him over, nearly lost balance himself, and they faced each other, staggering; but this lasted only a second; then the

23

father, panting and already screaming again, slumped down on the chair he had pulled close and dragged the son, who didn't resist any more, down till he lay prone across his knee, whereupon the father, pulling at the seat of the son's pants, let his hand smack down on the flat, slim buttocks of the son stretched taut under the shiny material of the pants, again and again, while his voice uttered completely unrecognizable words among yodeling cries. The son lay still, his hands hanging down to the floor; and the mother, accompanying each of the father's blows with a jerky movement of her back, was urging the son, and among her unclear, weeping words I distinguished these: now I ask, now you have to, now ask, otherwise you'll, he's already. With each word she moved a bit farther forward on the edge of the bed until only the final edge of her bottom was leaning against the final edge of the bed. The son now started whining in high, artificial gutturals, and although his mouth was pressed against the hollow of the father's knee I heard the words he cried in his strained, distorted voice: I won't do it again, I won't do it again, I'll never do it again, never, never do it again. The father was still hitting the son with weakening strokes and screamed words of which I got the following: well now, now at last, now you see, so at last, but before, never again, will you ever, can you, how shall I, how can I, will you really, have I now. His words, like his blows, became feebler and feebler till both words and blows died down and nothing but a rattling groan came from his mouth. The son turned his face and looked up at the father's face which had taken on a chalky hue with blue spots on temples and cheeks. The father pressed his left hand against his chest, at the heart, with his right he was fumbling at his collar-button; his eyes were closed, his mouth open with exhaustion. Groaning, he rubbed his chest; and the son slowly glided down from the father's knees, the eyes of his rigid, expressionless face fixed on the father's face. The mother had put the infant, who began yelling shrilly, down on the cover of the bed and ran with her arms spread wide to the father. The father stiffly kicked his legs forward and reared up over the back of the chair; the mother took his arms, tilted her face up and shouted words at the ceiling of which I caught these: you see, brought on, have done, O that you, you with your, can't stand. The son stood bending slightly forward with hanging shoulders and hands dangling at his knees; his eye had turned away from the father and fixed on the keyhole in the door as if he could see my eye in the darkness behind the keyhole. The mother, grabbing the father's head, kept on screaming while the father lay stiffly stretched across the chair, the heels of his boots propped on the floor, his back against the edge of the seat, the neck pressed against the back of the chair; and these are the words that were understandable among her stammering and screaming: O what's wrong, what's the matter, he done to you, O help help, not just look on, help help. She tried to turn the father's head and, when this failed, to loosen the father's hands, one of which was pressed against his heart, the other against his throat; and when this failed too, and the father kept lying across the chair, stiffly, with rattling breath, she hurried a few steps toward the door, turned around, tried the father's head and hands again, ran to the door again, and again back, shouting words of which I got these: O help help somebody, is nobody, anybody, don't let, help help, you've done, you've done, O help help. At these calls I opened the door and ran to the chair and put my hands under the father's shoulders and pulled him up, the mother helping by pushing from the back; we raised the stiff body up, but hardly was he upright when his knees, belly and neck bent, his hands fell down from the heart and throat, his arms dangled at the joints; the mother shouted: him to bed, quick bed; and so we dragged him between us to the bed; on the way to the bed, the mother pushed the son aside with an outward movement of her leg and shouted: you stand there, you look on, but help, is all. In front of the bed, she put the father in my arms with the words: hold him, just child aside; and I held the father, whose stale rattling breath wafted in my face, tightly until the mother had pushed the still bawling infant up on the pillow and turned to me again in order to lift the father's body onto the bed with me. While I let down his shoulders she pulled his legs from the floor and thus we put him on the bed lowering the upper part of his body and lifting the lower. Will end up killing him, the mother said to the son when the father was stretched out on the green cover, the red infant at his head, no longer crying but babbling curiously, diverted by the father's head beside him. The father opened his eyes and painfully turned his head sideways. The son sneaked over to the bed with hunched shoulders and, kneeling down in front of the bed, said as in a monotonous prayer: never again, never again, never do it again, never never doitagain; and the father lifted his hand and felt for the son's neck, ear, and part of the hair, and from there the hand slid down over the temple, the cheek, and the chin of the son, while he groaned deeply. The mother who was standing with folded hands at the head of the bed nodded at me and wiped her eyes; and I slowly went backward to the door; the beaten son was kneeling in front of the father's bed murmuring his prayer; and the father's breath was getting more regular, and his skin gradually returned from the chalky pallor to its natural coloring. With my hand stretched out behind me, I reached the door handle, pressed it down, opened the door, went out backward and shut the door in front of me.

Since I am, for the first time, getting my notes beyond a beginning that ends in nothing, I continue keeping to the sensations that crowd in on me here in my immediate surroundings; my hand guides the pencil over the paper, from word to word and from line to line, although I clearly feel the counterforce in me which used to get me to break off my attempts and which even now whispers with each row of words that I form according to what I have heard and seen, that what I've heard and seen is too insignificant to be preserved and that I'm wasting in this manner my hours, half my night, perhaps even all my day to no purpose; but I counter this with the question: what else shall I do; and from this question grows the insight that my other activities also remain without result or purpose. Tracing the occurrences in front of my eyes with my pencil in order to give an outline to what I've seen, to make what I've seen clearer, in short, to make seeing into an occupation, I sit next to the shed, on the stack of wood whose knotty pieces of root plastered with earth, moss and withered leaves give out a bitter rotten smell. From my high seat I survey the rutted, muddy plane of the yard still not dry from the last downpours, bordered by the long side of the house with the steps to the kitchen and the steps to the basement. Back of the house, the dirt road can be seen; it gets lost between the fields, but one can trace its course by the telephone poles, and these poles go, getting smaller and smaller and moving closer and closer to each other, as far as the misty curve of the horizon. Looking to my right, I see the pigsty, above its rim the pig's ears limply flapping back and forth, and the pig's tail curling up; next, the outhouse, brownish black, with slashed tar paper on the slanted roof; and a few hens are moving around the outhouse, picking in the earth and the meager islands of grass; between their picking and scratching, they make clucking sounds. Looking to the left, I notice the heap of stones behind the shed,

and behind the stone heap, the grange rises up surrounded
by wheel tracks; and behind the grange, the fields are
spread out; a horse is stamping along the furrows; and behind the horse, a plow is staggering, and behind the plow,
half supported on the handle of the plow, the hired man is
clomping; and back of the fields, there are woods in the
reddish purple haze, and low above the woods there is the
red sun breaking from steaming clouds, its light throwing
a long black purple shadow wherever it hits a shape rising
from the ground. The window to the family's room is
open; the father is leaning on the sill; he is stretching his
arms and his chest; and behind him the son can be seen,
his elbows on the table. The father's movements are strong
and full of expectation while the attitude of the son ex-
presses feebleness and resignation; the slight movements of
the mother's knees which, because of the limiting window
frame, are the only visible parts of her body make me think
that she is sitting on the edge of the bed and rocking the
infant in her arms. The kitchen door opens and Schnee
comes out, closes the door behind him and descends the
steps of the kitchen stairs. The father turns to the son,
takes hold of the son's wrist by swinging his arm backward,
and pulls the son to his side at the window. Between the
father and Mr. Schnee, the morning greeting takes place;
I cannot grasp the wording, but I recognize it from the
gestures: both nod their heads several times, the father
stretches his hand out of the window, and Mr. Schnee
reaches up to the window and takes the father's hand; they
shake hands; then the father's head turns back and forth
between Schnee and the son, and also his hand goes back
and forth between the son and Schnee, from which I conclude that the father is repeating his offer of yesterday and
wants to see it in effect. And sure enough he pushes the
son up to the windowsill right after, Schnee raises his arms
toward the son, and the son jumps down to him. Schnee

and the son go side by side to the stones next to the house;
Schnee's arm is resting on the son's shoulders.

The son, having under Schnee's direction gathered small
and large stones from various places and filled the wheelbarrow with them (which actually neither helped Schnee
nor saved him time since he bent down for every stone
together with the son, having first pointed it out with his
finger, then felt the stone with his fingers after the son
had picked it up, and turned to watch the stone while the
son put it on the heap, and bent over it again once it was
on the heap, and with both hands took hold of the shovel
which the son thrust into the heap of stones, and then lifted
the shovel together with the son, or rather, lifted the shovel
himself, its weight increased by the son's arms, and emptied
the shovel into the wheelbarrow, dragging the son's hands
and arms along on the shovel), came toward me with the
wheelbarrow. Schnee had delegated this transfer of the
stones to him; Schnee only followed him with his eyes,
rounding his hands as if he himself were holding the
handles and straining forward as if he himself were pushing the barrow. The son pushed the barrow toward me,
bent over the handles with all his strength; he not only had
to push the weight of the barrow forward through the
mud, but also to balance the weight, always ready to sink
to the left or right, in the middle over the wheel. He pushed
the barrow toward me; and thick lumps of mud gathered
on the wheel whose spokes half disappeared in the mud;
mud also gathered on the son's shoes, white rubbers full of
holes, and mud splattered his pants up to the knees. In order
to get to the stone heap behind the shed, however, the son
had to curve to the left with the barrow or, from the son's
point of view, to the right; but he came straight toward me
steering the barrow with difficulty; even when I pointed

29

my hand to the left to draw his attention to the direction
he had to take, he continued his way toward me; I waved
my hand more violently and kept my arm stretched out to
the left, but the wheel kept turning through the mud right
at me. Schnee, back at the house, stretched out his right arm
and pointed to the right; thus we both pointed in the same
direction, Schnee by pointing to the right, and I by pointing to the left, the direction the son had to take in order to
get to the stone heap; but the son pushed the barrow up to
the wood stack; in front of the wood stack, right under my
feet, he set it down. The son straightened up and looked at
me; I was still holding my arm stretched to the left. The
son turned to Schnee who was still holding his right arm
stretched out; and in this moment, while the son turned to
Schnee and back to the barrow and put his hands back on
the handles and tensed his muscles to lift the barrow,
I surveyed once more, still more exactly than before, the
buildings and constituent parts of the landscape around
me; I saw the tiles on the roof of the house shining in a
moist, deep red, the weathervane on the chimney, and the
thin bluish smoke rising from the chimney, and I saw the
crystalline gleaming of grains of sand on the ground, and,
on the horizon, a second cloud of smoke perhaps from a
hunter's campfire or from a burning shed, and a rabbit
hopping through the furrows, and the grass and thistles
growing rankly on the fallow fields. Now the son had lifted
the barrow and wanted to turn it to one side; the wheel
had sunk into the mud up to the hub; he pulled and pushed,
and, back at the house, Schnee pulled and pushed the air
in front of him with rounded hands (his right arm had
come down); but the barrow moved neither back nor forward, it only tilted to the right and to the left until, after
a violent tug, it tipped over and with a rumble discharged
its load. The son stood still for a while and looked down at
the stones. The father leaned out of the window of the

family's room and shouted words of which I got: do a job
and show you; he gesticulated wildly with raised fist; and
the son knelt down and began to put the stones one by one
back into the barrow. I climbed down from the stack of
wood and knelt beside the son in the soft mud and helped
him fill the barrow with stones; and when the barrow was
full I grasped the handles together with the son and pushed
the barrow, in a concerted effort with the son, past the
stack of wood toward the shed, and then past the shed to
the stone heap. At the stone heap, we raised the handles
and threw the stones from the barrow on the heap; and
then the son turned the empty barrow and, by himself,
pushed it along the rut back to Schnee who was waiting
for him with dangling arms and who, after the son had
joined him, continued his activities of bending down, picking up, gathering and loading. The father, leaning far out
of the window with his arms folded on the sill, watched
these activities. He watched the son bending over the stones
together with Schnee and putting the stones in a heap and
then thrusting the shovel into the heap and emptying the
shovel into the barrow; and I also, back on the stack of
wood, watched these activities when I noticed that, for
some moments, even the housekeeper, who, upstairs in the
house, had opened the window of her room in order to
shake out her sheets, was watching these activities after
having shaken the sheets; thus Schnee's and the son's activities were the focal point of our lines of vision. When
the wheelbarrow was again filled with stones the son took
the handles and pushed the barrow along the rut toward
me. This time the wheel turned more easily since the mud
was pressed firm in the groove, but this time the son had
a harder time keeping the barrow balanced and I explained
this to myself thus: when, the last time, the son was pushing the barrow through the more resistant mud, he had
leaned more heavily over the handles and the middle axis

31 🦋

of the barrow and had thus counteracted the tendency of
the weight to tilt to the right or to the left, while now,
when he was steering the total weight of the barrow just
from the farthest ends of the handles, he had a heavier and
more independent mass in front of him. I waved my hand,
stretching it toward him and pulling it back, thus trying to
suggest that he should lean farther toward the center of
the barrow; and back at the house, Schnee, following the
son with his eyes, made a gesture with his hand that started
from his chest and went toward the son. But the son who
only paid attention to keeping the wheel of the barrow in
the rut made by the wheel didn't pay attention to my gesture and didn't turn to Schnee either which is how he could
have noticed Schnee's motioning; he pushed the barrow
toward me, only supporting it right and left with his outstretched arms until he, right in front of the stacked wood,
reached the spot where he, last time, had wanted to turn
the barrow; and here the track had been hollowed out by
the weight and the turning back and forth of the barrow;
and the wheel got bogged in this hole; and the son's body
was too far from the barrow to be able to keep the barrow,
which was already tilting from too one-sided a pushing at
the handles and from the increased pressure of stones rolling to that side, from tipping over; and so the barrow tipped
over, at the same place as before.

I couldn't muster the energy to describe again how I
climbed down from the stack of wood and helped the son
pick up the stones; instead, after having written this last
paragraph of my observations, after having gone to my
room after picking up the stones, I lay down, lay down on
my bed, put a few grains of salt in my eyes and saw, after a
short blurred stage, a picture in front of me; or rather, I
glided into the picture; I felt as if I were moving along a

road, a wide asphalt road; I felt as if I were reclining comfortably in a car, a bus (I couldn't see the vehicle, it consisted only of a feeling of motion, of gliding), and while I was gliding along evenly and restfully, I saw, as far as the eye could reach, elk or deer lying along the road, huge animals, in pairs, copulating; the heads with the enormous antlers were raised high and from the gaping mouths rose the steam of hot breath. The hooves of each male animal hit the female shoulders and breast in a rough caress; and the rhythmic movements of the heavy bodies were accompanied by a hollow, giggly rattling from all the throats. While I glided along the unending row of animals the picture dissolved and the outlines of the room showed through. Looking at the outlines of the room through the still moving shadows of the animals, I heard, still listening for the sound of the bony clash of antlers, a knock at the door; and the knock washed away the last bits of the picture and made the room, with its walls, its objects, its window and its door come into focus, and after the knock, the door opened without my answering the knock; and the doctor entered the room, supporting himself on a cane, shut the door behind him and leaned against the wall fingering the bandaged and plastered spots on his head and face. His lips were moving, but I could not hear his voice; I sat up and put my hand to my ear, but there wasn't even a whisper; then I got up and went close to him and put my ear directly to his mouth, and now I could make out the following words from his breath and his tongue-motions: wounds not heal, whichever way I cut, hollow out deeply, down to the bone, knife on the bone, grates, scrapes, breaks off, sits deeper yet, bandage, all night, all night awake, still blood, pus, farther, down at the arm, then farther up, lifted, armpit, humerus, boil water, sprain, pain, bind, find, to the ribs, in the breast, deep in the breast, heart laid bare, lung, legs, plaster cast around the ankles, saws, clean cut, round the calves, shinbone cut, tendons, plaster cast knee-high, thigh, deep in the abdomen, two pots of pus and blood, further in fury, and now (here he took his black glasses off, and his eyes were staring ahead with an empty, whitish shimmer) nothing more to see, even the strongest light, all in the dark, keep on, cutting in the dark, poise the knife, slide, widen, grope, tap, overlap, instruments lost, lost, lost, in the dark, swabs dropping, find ether, clamps, needle, thread, wound open, at random, arm all slashed, lose direction, lose the door, the table, wrong door, don't know upstairs, downstairs, up or down, sit in the dark, don't know arm or leg, pain the same, same pain, everywhere, wherever cut the same pain, drive out pain, drown out, sing against; here he raised his voice and started to bray half groaning and gnashing his teeth, brayed, played, blade, brayed against the blade, by song allayed, blood and voice be stayed. I supported his arm, opened the door, led him out of my room, shut the door behind us, led him through the garret to the stairs, and on the way he kept braying: where, where does he lead me, he the patient me the doctor, where, where does he lead me, where, where does the patient lead the doctor; and when we had reached the stairs and I went down backward before him, holding his arms and guiding his stiff feet, he kept on braying: where, where, to the stair, the stair, down the stair, down the down zigzag stair, zigzag down the stair, down the downy stair, a wall here and a wall there, we crawl along the wall, wall to the hall, we crawl along the hall wall. Having reached the hall I led him along the hall to the door of his room, and on this bit of the way he brayed: now on the plain, how bear the pain, life will remain, life will remain, who is with me, who is holding me, the patient, the patient the doctor; and when we had gotten to his door and I had pressed the handle down and led him into his room, he sang: open the door, open to the core, cut the sore, the pain gets more, and more and more, d'you hear the roar, who, who is with me, who in the room, what room, who, who; and when I had shut the door of his room behind us and led him to his bed and made him sit down, his braying faded into a monotonous *oooo* growing weaker and weaker and finally dying down. The four walls, the floor and the ceiling forming his room are furnished in such a way that, upon entering, one sees a long, coarse wooden table, so rough that it seems put together by the doctor's own hands, jutting out from right next to the door into the middle of the room where it touches a second table going to the right in a right angle which again touches a third table jutting out to the left in a right angle, nearly up to the window-wall opposite the door so that only a narrow space is left between the table and the wall; one can just squeeze through sideways, but with difficulty, and in doing so pass a window to the left, a small, high, round table full of tweezers, scalpels, needles, glasses, bottles, bowls and boxes that immediately joins a second such table, whereupon one is faced by three chairs stacked high with books, whereupon one turns to the right since the wall that forms right angles with the window-wall and the door-wall blocks the way; thus one leaves the just mentioned wall to the left and sees to the right, in the space between this wall and the rectangularly joined tables, a small, low, square table with a bowl of blood and, behind this table, a second, somewhat higher square table covered with bloody and pus-filled wads of cotton, whereupon one has reached the door-wall and can either turn back to the window-wall or climb under the first long table in order to get to the door again; in thought, I chose the latter, in order to examine the left half of the room, again starting from the door; there one finds first a high cabinet with glass doors, its shelves filled with innumerable brown, green and black labeled bottles as well as with boxes, packages, and bags labeled or at least written on, stamped, and numbered;

whereupon one notices a leather armchair with some iodine-
stained towels on the seat and the back, and then the iron
bed painted white, after which just the bedside table at
the head of the bed, also crammed with bottles, tubes, and
boxes, has to be mentioned to complete the inventory of
the doctor's room. In this room I stood now, after having
set the doctor down on the bed, in front of the doctor's
swaying body until the housekeeper, down in the hall, hit
a spoon against the lid of a pot which was the signal for
breakfast, whereupon two doors in the hall opened, the
tailor's and the captain's, and I could hear, outside the
house, the heavy, clomping steps of the hired man who
must have moved with the horse from the field to the stable
and from the stable to the kitchen door long before the
housekeeper's signal, probably after having several times
pulled out and snapped open his pocket watch, as well as
the mother's voice calling the son from the window of the
family's room, and Mr. Schnee's steps coming up from the
yard toward the kitchen steps, and then my and the doctor's steps, since I had pulled the doctor up from the bed
and led him again through the room to the door and from
there, after having opened the door and closed it behind us,
through the hall and down the stairs and through the hall
to the kitchen where, with our arrival, all participants in
the meal were gathered. Before we all sat down at the table,
the housekeeper came up to the captain and lifted her
pointed fingers to his back in order to remove a long, white
thread sticking to his jacket in a wavy line. She picked the
thread up, showed it to the captain who bent down and
looked at it, and carried it to the sink where she let it drop;
slowly it sank down. Now we sat down, took a slice each
of the already cut bread, spread lard on it, and started eating it with the coffee the housekeeper poured from the blue
pot into our mugs. Again the tailor's appetite was notice-
able although the tailor had just left his bedroom, whereas

the rest of us, except for the captain, had already spent a few hours moving around, partly in the house and partly outside; as for gobbling down his slice of bread, he nearly outdid the hired man who reeked with the smell of the plowed field. But when he tried to be the first to turn to a second slice, he suddenly stopped, froze in a gesture of surprise, reached into his mouth, and pulled out a tooth that must have loosened from his lower jaw during his violent chewing. He held the tooth in front of himself and stared at it. The captain said: a tooth. The housekeeper also said: a tooth. Mr. Schnee held his hand across the table under the tailor's hand holding the tooth and said: give me. The tailor lowered the tooth into Schnee's hand, Schnee took the tooth, wiped it with his handgerchief, looked at it and put it into the upper pocket of his jacket, saying: also teeth in my collection. The tailor put back the slice of bread he had already taken and sat immobile. The hired man ate on unconcerned. The doctor chewed his bread with difficulty. Mr. Schnee ate on. The housekeeper ate on. I ate on in order to stifle the suddenly rising feeling that this morning would never end.

Occasionally, when it is the birthday of one of the boarders, or on a holiday marked red in the calendar, or on any other day if she feels like it, the housekeeper invites us in the evening to a party in her room. It happened this evening. After supper, during which the housekeeper had invited us to visit her room, and after the family had been called too, everybody went to her room to drink his mug of coffee. Everyone went across the threshold holding the mug that had been filled with coffee in the kitchen, and went to the back of the room, passing first, to the right, an oval table with a lace tablecloth and a big purple glass vase, and, to the left, a chest of drawers with photographs of

older and younger women, young girls, a child playing
with a hoop, a baby on its belly, older and younger men,
partly unbearded, partly with mustaches and beards, then
walking along the back of a couch jutting out into the room
on the one hand, and a square, also lace-covered table bearing a china statue, a shepherdess in crinoline with three
sheep and a jumping dog, on the other, whereupon he went
by, on the left, the tall column of a parchment-shaded
lamp, and, on the right, by a low table, next to the couch,
with round brass top on which there were a crystal bowl
filled with colored balls of wool, a shell-covered box, a
brass candleholder with a candle, not burning however, an
inkpot, and an iron; in order to turn either to the right and
be faced by two deeply cushioned armchairs, a high, black
chair with corkscrew back posts, and another, silk-cov-
ered, oval table with a flesh-colored china dancer with bare
breasts and legs and a loose gown, as well as a realistically
colored wooden fawn and a cordial bottle and ten glasses
on it, or to the left where he could see a wicker chair, a
round table with a lamp with a silk shade, a leather armchair, a hassock, a footstool, a bedside table with marble
top, a comb, scissors, a bowl of lard, a few hair curlers and
a little potbellied bottle partly lying, partly standing on it.
and the bed covered with a white woolen blanket. Aside
from these chairs and tables among which we were now
scattered, there were more things and pieces of furniture
along the walls; the foot of the bed touched a washstand
with a china water bowl and water jug, a glass with a
toothbrush, a soapholder, a hairbrush, a finger brush, and
some hairpins; above the washstand there was a mirror
reflecting some of the furniture and some of the guests;
next to the washstand stood a high wardrobe with closed
doors; above the bed was a picture showing a boar being
chased by dogs and attacked by hunters armed with spears
in the thick of a forest, and a second picture at the head of

the bed, of a basket filled with violets. Once the eye had gone along the window which was framed by long heavy drapes of dark blue velvet and had a low table full of potted plants in front of it, it came to a treelike growth planted in a bucket, with large sword-shaped leaves nearly reaching the ceiling, to another round, lace-covered table with a lamp that had a shade of glass beads and a music box, to another chest of drawers filled with photographs also showing older and younger men and women, here a house, there the bay of a sea with a piece of beach and a few beach-chairs among big round pebbles, here a high railway bridge across a ravine, there a monument of a horse and a horseman, here a lookout rising above trees, and there a wide avenue of a city, to a half-open closet door, to a carved black chair with high back over which a picture showed snowy, moonlit hills, as well as, finally, to another table, of wicker, bearing a big empty vase of grainy clay painted with flowers. The housekeeper, who had entered the room first, filled nine of the ten glasses with the green cordial from the bottle, after having put down her coffee cup on the table with the bottle, and handed a glass to each of the guests who, from all sides, each held out one arm toward her; because of the distance and hindering pieces of furniture between, many of the guests could not reach the glass in her hand, but had to take it from the hand of one of the others, or from the hands of several of the other guests standing between the remote guest and the housekeeper; this caused a good deal of bowing forward and bowing to the side of the upper parts of the bodies of those present, a circling, reaching out and drawing back of arms, until everybody had gotten his glass, and only one single empty glass was standing beside the bottle. The housekeeper and the mother sat down on the couch; opposite, in the deep armchairs, the captain and Mr. Schnee were sitting, and, on the high, black chair, the father, while the doctor sank into the leather armchair, looking at the housekeeper's and the mother's backs and at the back of the couch, and the hired man chose the hassock, and the tailor the footstool for a seat. I myself was standing at the window, the mug in one hand, the glass in the other; and the son, who had not gotten a glass (it was the father who had forbidden it; the housekeeper would certainly, as it happened once before, at just such a gathering as to-day's, have filled the last empty glass and handed it to him, if the father's interference hadn't kept her from doing so), was standing beside me, one hand around his mug, the other cramped in the drapes, in the drapes which he looked up at, tugging as if to test how solid they were. Of the words the housekeeper, whose thighs were forced under the low table, said to the mother who, hampered by the edge of the oval table jutting over the back of the couch, was leaning diagonally toward the housekeeper, I understood the following fragments: cook beans thoroughly, ham, rind of bacon, melt fat, solid fat, lard, hole (whole); whereupon I heard the mother say, while lifting her glass and sipping at it: if sleeping, kicks off, blanket slides, diapers wet, wakes me, milk gives out, always sucking, today beans too (bean stew). Of the captain's words addressed to Mr. Schnee, his legs crossed, sipping alternately at the mug and the glass, I caught: enjoy leisure, right at rest, rare in former times, as at that time; to which I heard Schnee answer, who had put his mug on the table in front of him and was turning the liqueur glass in his big, bony hands: work quite different (were quite different), something different, point is, gathered together; whereupon the father turned to him with the following audible words, pulling his chair close to Schnee's armchair: relieved, in spite of all not that easy, clumsy, sneaks, spokes, always stumbling(tumbling), all the time stumbling, sure taken him to task. Schnee answered: of course satisfied, I would, strange, getting started is half, always hard battle, all a matter of patience, without patience, together gathered collection together; his other words got lost in the rising giggle of the housekeeper exclaiming: there you could, some man; which the mother complemented with the words: count to twenty, bridegrooms aplenty; whereupon the housekeeper muttered something that escaped me because at that moment the tailor turned to the doctor with the following clear words: feel better, much better when weather better, in the back too, always, get it in the back, before weather changes, rain over, long enough, always the back, once two years ago, no two, no two and a half years, so I couldn't get up, no three years, get it in back, still farther back, last year too, also the back, now better, sun all afternoon. The doctor, the glass at his barely moving lips, spoke very low: no improvement, not yet, expect any improvement, indifferent, what matter, what, yet, but gnawing; drowned out by the words the hired man said to both the doctor and the tailor: can confirm (cancan firm), field the afternoon, wear me out, clouds, get clear, tell by clouds, in the wrists and knees too, had an uncle, drops he (dropsy, drop see), couldn't move; then again a few laughing words from the housekeeper hit my ear: so tasty, but tasty, had it at the station hotel, that time at the station hotel, couldn't imagine better, or hardly; the mother's laughing cut out the next words of which I got only: shouldn't say, you know, understand; and the mother added, with a side glance at the father: back forth, back forth, drill, keep trying, fizzle, out; and these words, in turn, got drowned in the housekeeper's laughter. From the hired man I then heard: still had the cow, leading the bull, cart coming, was the coachman, still coming, lift block, bull out, smelled already, foam at the mouth, crash with the horns, held the cow, didn't want, tied up, tail, ram in; at which the doctor leaned over to the hired man and asked:

41

was cow long ago, never seen, before my time; to which the hired man answered: miscarriage, slaughtered, loss, not worth it, farming, without help, strength, wrack and ruin; here the doctor said, opening the safety pin of his head bandage: several years ago, or months; and then, calling over to the housekeeper: how long actually here, when did come. The housekeeper wasn't listening; she said to the mother: take up (take cup), sew up, hem up, put on collar (color), show skirt, wear hat, go to town, often intend, never get around; whereupon the mother pointed at the closet and said: ostrich feather, wonderful white, be smart, dancing, with music; whereupon the housekeeper called over to the son: wind the box, music box, wind, key inside, hear music. The son hunched over the music box and turned the key to wind the creaky works. I heard the spring beginning to crack inside the box, and I was already lifting my hand to warn him that he mustn't turn any more if he didn't want to break the spring, but it was too late; hardly had I lifted my hand than there was a snapping sound, followed by a short clattering and rattling; the son was standing motionless, his hand on the key. The house-keeper jumped up knocking over a half-full coffee mug; the coffee ran over the table and into the lap of the mother who couldn't move away fast enough; the housekeeper heaved herself sideways past the father, Schnee and the captain and hit the glass the captain was holding in front of himself; and the contents of the glass, only a few drops, it is true, ran down the lapel of his cutaway; the mother, shaking her skirt and squeezing by the table, caught her foot on the leg of the table, losing her shoe; then she stumbled toward the father who had time enough to open his arms to catch her, but not time to put down the mug in one hand and the glass in the other, which made both coffee and liqueur splatter over both the mother's dress and the father's pants. The housekeeper, her hands ready

to grab the key to the music box (which was to come
loose in her hand), in sweeping by caught the iron on the
table with the bow of her apron strings; and the iron fell on
something which had been withdrawn the moment the
housekeeper ran by, but which immediately pushed forward again: Mr. Schnee's foot; and the iron striking drew
a loud scream from him, whereupon he bent all the way
down over his hurt foot and blew, with a whistling sound,
on the shoe. The housekeeper had now reached the key,
with her hands far ahead of her and her legs still a jump
behind; the son had let go of the key and retreated; the key
turned, as I had expected, loosely in the box without resistance. Box kaputt, the housekeeper cried: take to town,
repair. The father screamed: right now, tonight, take, get
to town tomorrow morning, right away to the locksmith,
right away, get the lead out, all night. I took the music box
and the key which had slipped out into the housekeeper's
hand and handed the music box and the key to the son; the
son, his head on his chest, looked at me from below, with
the bluish white of his eyeballs shining around the black
iris, then he went hastily, the box under his arm and the
key in his hand, through the room, past the back of the
couch, the tables and the chest of drawers, opened the door,
stepped out, closed the door behind him, and went away
through the hall and down the stairs. We could still hear
the kitchen door snapping shut. In the room, the talking
started up again after the silence which accompanied the
son's departure. There was talk about the broken music
box, about the iron, about Mr. Schnee's foot, about the
spilled coffee and liqueur, about the spots in the clothes,
and after a while, the lines of thought began to branch
out more and more from the events which had just happened: from the words of the housekeeper and the mother,
who had both returned to the couch, the housekeeper from
the table where the music box had been, and the mother

from the father's lap where she had sat down, one could conclude that they were talking about aprons, blouses, skirts, bonnets, ribbons, and hats; and from the words of Mr. Schnee who was again leaning back in his armchair, and the words of the captain, who had wiped the stain on his vest with his handkerchief, I could make out that they were speaking of pressed pants, shoe models, polished and unpolished shoes, riding boots, horses, and a wine cellar in the garrison town; and from the remarks which the father made, whose face had turned a bluish red during the accident with the music box and returned to its natural color after the son had disappeared, I could understand that they were about corporal punishment, running the gauntlet, hanging, decapitating, imprisonment, drowning, burning, and banishment. The circle of conversations ran on and on and blended into a general though diversified buzzing, while the doctor, who had hardly paid attention to the incident of the music box, but had gone on unrolling his head bandage with one hand and rolling it into a ball with the other, loosened the last bloody, sticky piece of bandage from his forehead, and while the hired man, with a throaty cooing, pulled the cards from his pocket, shuffled the cards, and divided them between himself and the tailor who had moved his footstool closer to the hired man. The hired man threw a few cards on the floor in front of him and said: a jack and a nine; and the tailor threw a card beside the cards on the floor and said: a three; and the hired man right away threw two new cards beside the cards on the floor and exclaimed: a king and a two; whereupon the tailor threw two of his cards next to the cards on the floor crying: king and ace. The exhausted doctor was leaning his head against the back of the armchair; on his forehead, a large, festering wound was showing which he touched lightly and cautiously with the little finger of his left hand. The housekeeper and the mother got up, talking about dress hems,

mother-of-pearl buttons, corset hooks, hat pins and
brooches, and, smoothing their dresses with their hands,
went sideways past the oval table, past the father's chair,
past the wicker table with the clay lamp, and past the
other empty, black chair to the closet door, slid the closet
door open completely, and went into the clothes-filled
space, the housekeeper first, the mother pulling the door
shut behind them as she crossed the threshold. Hardly had
the door clicked shut than we heard muted shouting
from within among which the following words were recognizable: lock, get open, push, pull, locked in, whereupon
there were knocks against the inside of the door. All but
the doctor turned toward the closet door, remaining, however, seated a few moments longer while the knocking
grew stronger, then, having caught on to what had
happened, they jumped up, the father first, the captain
second, Schnee third, the hired man fourth, the tailor last
(I stayed at the window), and ran as fast as they could
between the chairs, tables, lamps, chests, and plants to the
closet door. Where is the key, the father shouted at the
door which the captain's fist hit at the same moment; the
key, where is it, he shouted once more, but with the captain's knocking one couldn't hear the answer from within.
The father got hold of the captain's hand and shouted
once again: where key; and from within the hollow answer:
is no key. Is no key, the captain asked back from the outside, and while incomprehensible words were shouted
from the inside, the father repeated: no key. Where the
key, the hired man called, and Schnee said to the hired
man: is no key, key gone, while the housekeeper's voice
behind the door shouted something incomprehensible. Is
key gone, the father called to the door, and from the inside we could hear indistinctly: key gone, break open,
suffocating; and the father shouted: break door open or
will suffocate, and already was throwing his weight force-

fully against the door which, however, did not give in to his barrage. Then the captain threw himself against the door which resisted him as well, and it also resisted the hired man and Mr. Schnee who rushed against the door together. Get an ax, said the father, and the hired man called to the door, get the ax, wait, just to the shed, get the ax, then he turned around, ran past the wicker table with the vase and the oval table with the vase, climbed over the couch and ran to the door, opened the door, left it open behind him, ran through the hall, downstairs, through the downstairs hall, through the kitchen, threw open the kitchen door, ran out, leaving the kitchen door open behind him, down the steps and across the yard to the shed; I saw him crossing the streak of light that was falling on the ground from the window. In the closet, the mother and the housekeeper were screaming and hitting the door; and outside, the father, the captain, Mr. Schnee, and the tailor were screaming at the door: back right away, calm down, just the ax, be back right away, cut door open, right away, open right away. Then the hired man came from the shed, came running from the dark into the streak of light from the window, flew up the steps to the kitchen door, over the threshold of the kitchen door, pulled the kitchen door shut behind him, ran through the kitchen, the hall, up the stairs, along the hall, and into the room, slamming the door behind him. He jumped across the couch one hand supported on the back, the other waving the ax. The father reached for the ax, and the hired man shoved the ax toward him, then the father lifted the ax, while all the others drew back from the door, and called: I'm going to chop now, and drove the ax into the lock of the door. The ax went deep into the wood. The hired man helped the father, who was laboriously tugging at the handle, to pull the ax out of the wood; then the father drove the ax again into the door, tugged again, with the hired man helping, at the ax which had sunk deep into the wood; but this time the ax did not come out, but broke off at the head of the shaft. In the closet, the housekeeper and the mother, who had calmed down during the work, were again pounding against the door and shouting words of which I caught: hot and air (scared). Mr. Schnee lifted his hand and cried: go for the crowbar, and ran between the chairs and tables, past the couch and the chest of drawers, to the door, opened the door, leapt over the threshold leaving the door open behind him, disappeared through the hall, the stairs, the downstairs hall, the kitchen, the kitchen door which he left open behind him, and the kitchen steps, popped up in the streak of light below the window, and disappeared again in the dark. Just go to the bar, the father shouted at the door, and the captain shouted: gone for the crowbar; just gone for the crowbar, the father shouted, right back, break the door open, ax broken, break the door with the bar with crowbar; and the housekeeper cried inside, behind the door: heat, stifling. Schnee with the crowbar appeared in the light, ran through the brightness, up the kitchen stairs, through the kitchen door which he left open behind him, through the kitchen, the hall, up the stairs, along the hall, and appeared, the crowbar raised high in his hand, on the threshold which he leapt across, slamming the door behind him, racing past the furniture in a curve through the room to the closet door. The hired man took the crowbar from him and thrust it, together with the father, between the jamb and the door; and they shoved and tugged at the crowbar until the wood of the door started to crack and splinter. After they had rammed the crowbar several times into the splitting wood around the lock and pulled it out again with combined strength, and driven it in between the door and the jamb, the door began to loosen; the wood bent, apparently under the weight of the bodies of the housekeeper and the mother

47 🔏

pressing from inside, and finally the door split open, didn't give way to one side, however, but, having slid off the hinges, fell forward, on the father's head. He staggered backward, and at the same time the housekeeper and the mother staggered out of the closet, over the door into the room. In the hurly-burly of simultaneous movements, the hired man bent over the door, and Schnee over the crowbar, the father rubbed his head, the housekeeper and the mother stumbled to the couch, the hired man lifted the door and Schnee the crowbar, the housekeeper and the mother sat down on the couch, the tailor picked up wood splinters from the floor, the father put a pillow on his head, the hired man leaned the door against the closet jamb, Schnee put the crowbar in the corner to the right of the closet, the captain filled his glass, the housekeeper lifted the captain's coffee mug and the mother the housekeeper's coffee mug, the father tottered past the chairs with the pillow on his head, the captain emptied his glass, the housekeeper and the mother slurped what was left in the mugs, the doctor, who even during the incident with the closet door had been sitting unconcerned in his armchair, his head leaning back, got up, the father moved past the big, sword-leaved plant and me, the tailor picked up the splinters he had gathered into a heap, the doctor went through the room with the rolled-up bandage in one hand, leaning on the backs of the chairs, the couch, and the chest of drawers with the other, the father opened the window and, catching hold of the drapes with one hand, leaned out of the window, the housekeeper and the mother leaned back on the couch, Schnee sat down in his armchair, the doctor opened the door, the hired man went to the cards spread out on the floor, the tailor went between the pieces of furniture through the room with the wood splinters under his arm, the doctor left the room, pulling the door shut behind him, the father straightened up, pulling at the drapes, the captain balanced on his toes, his hands on his back under his tails, the drapes, probably loosened already by the son's tugging, together with the curtain rod and the wood around it, fell down hitting the father's head and knocking down the potted plants, the father scrambled out from under the cloth of the drapes, the housekeeper, followed by the mother, jumped up from the couch, the tailor dropped his wood at the door, the hired man looked up from the cards and at the window, the captain ran past Schnee to the father, kicking chairs and stools aside, Mr. Schnee got out of his armchair, the mother, squeezing by between Schnee and the table, took the father's arm, the hired man walked over to the knocked-down pots, I stretched my arm into the cold draft from outside and shut the window, the mother put her arm around the father and led him through the furniture to the door, the tailor bent over the fallen wood, Schnee sank back into his chair, the hired man picked up the pots with a throaty hum, the captain and I picked up the wood molding with the curtain rod and the drapes on it, the housekeeper and the hired man put the pots back on the plant table, the mother opened the door, the tailor picked up the wood, the mother and the father crossed the threshold, the captain and I rolled up the drapes, the housekeeper went sideways by the armchairs, grazing Schnee's head, and by the chest with the photographs to the closet, the captain and I put the drapes with the rod and the wood around it in the corner next to the chest of drawers, the housekeeper brought a broom from the closet, the mother shut the door behind herself and the father, the captain returned to his armchair, the tailor straightened up with the picked-up wood, Mr. Schnee filled his glass, the tailor opened the door, the housekeeper with the broom came to the window, the captain poured himself more liqueur from the bottle, the tailor crossed the threshold, the housekeeper swept the earth spilled from the pots, the tailor shut the door behind him, the hired man went back to the cards, the captain lifted the glass to his mouth, I went by the tables, the chairs, the back of the couch, the chest of drawers, to the door, the hired man picked the cards up from the floor, I opened the door, the wood of the housekeeper's broom hit the wall and the legs of the plant table, I crossed the threshold and shut the door behind me.

The day following this night I spent, until dusk, describing the evening which I have just finished describing. Sitting at the table in my room I look through the garret window and see beyond the edge of the sloping roof a piece of the muddy yard limited by the wood stack, the woodshed, the heap of stones, and the grange. In the moist purple furrows, the hired man is clomping behind the plow pulled by the horse; and over the broken earth a crow is flapping which, because of its single cry (which, as I now remember, I had heard earlier today while writing) I suspect to be the same crow I had heard crying harm over the fields two days ago when I started writing. The sky above the woods beyond the fields back of the plowing hired man is a burning, bloody red; the shadow of the hired man, the plow, and the horse is lying long and wavy on the furrows beneath the fluttering shadow of the crow; the shadow of the house goes up to the wood stack, the shed, and the heap of stones; beside it, long and narrow, the shadow of the outhouse, and the shadow of the grange is spread hugely over the fields, topped by the shadow of a human figure. The man throwing the shadow on the roof of the grange is the father who, his legs clamped around the ridge, is watching the dirt road with binoculars in spite of the repeated call echoing against the wall of the grange and coming most likely from the mother leaning out of the window of the family's room: much much too early early, won't be back back for a long a long time. I can tell the passage of time by the sky changing from burning red to rust brown, and by the shadows creeping farther out into the fields and blurring their outlines. Then, within a few seconds (the sun sinks behind the horizon opposite) the shadows spill inkily over the ground; the hired man is up to his knees in darkness, only his face is still glowing red; and the darkness climbs up the wall of the grange whose roof is still reflecting the last of the sunlight; then the hired man's face is extinguished, and then the roof of the grange; the father's face and the shiny metal knob of the binoculars stay longest in the sun, until even the colors of the father's face and the binoculars grow dull, and everything is covered in a single gloomy shadow, the shadow of the earth. Now the father raises his arm and, pointing toward the dirt road, turns to the house and shouts, probably to the mother he no doubt sees in the window: it's coming, the coach, the coach is coming. I raise the window and lean out and see, far back on the dirt road, something dark approaching slowly and gradually taking the shape of a coach with a horse.

As always at the approach of the coach, announced from afar by the coachman's horn signal, the boarders, except for the doctor who stayed at the threshold of the kitchen door, went out in front of the house and gathered by the side of the road in order to wait there for the coach, together with the housekeeper and the hired man who both had left their work, whatever it was, as they always did for the arrival of the coach, and had gone to the middle of the road. In the growing darkness, the horse moved toward us, not galloping and not running, but in a slow trot, and behind it the reeling coach with the coachman's outline high on the box; and the speed or slowness of the approach was in exact proportion to the increasing darkness, so that the coach would have been swallowed by the dark had it stood still, but since it moved, it constantly balanced the degree of increased darkness by the degree of approaching speed, but it also stayed blurred because of the increasing darkness, so that, when it finally stood right in front of us, it had gained only in size, but was still just as foglike and smoldering, just as embedded in the deep dusk as before. The previous moment of the coachman's tightening the reins and telling the horse to stop with the drumming sound of his tongue was three days and three nights ago, three days and three nights in which I couldn't bring myself to continue my notes because of an absolute indifference; and even now I can only continue with difficulty the description of the coach's arrival and what followed, ready to break off at any moment and to give it up for good. After the stopping of the horse, three days and three nights ago, the coachman got down from the box, greeting the house-keeper by shaking hands with her, greeting the hired man by waving his hand at him, and greeting the rest of us by nodding at us, except for the doctor, back at the front door whom he didn't notice. He was dressed in a wide leather coat, and wore a broad-rimmed felt hat with a few dappled partridge feathers stuck in the band. His legs, in polished boots of brown leather, walked as if they had springs in the hollow of the knee. His horn was hanging on a strap over his shoulder. The father and the mother opened the door of the coach, leaned far into it, turned away and walked back to the house, shaking their heads. The hired man too looked into the coach; he thrust in his arms and pulled out a sack, filled with coal to judge by the external shape; it could also have been filled with potatoes, but this possibility was ruled out since the house had its own potato field and, for that reason, didn't need to order potatoes from the town. Bending his knees, the hired man pressed his back against the sack, raised his hands over his shoulders, lowered them behind his shoulders, grabbed the sack, straightened his legs, bent forward holding the sack on his back, and went toward the kitchen steps, past the kitchen steps and toward the basement steps, down the basement steps to the basement door which he kicked open. The coachman also reached into the coach and pulled out a sack, bent his knees, pulled the sack onto his back with his arms raised high, straightened his leather-rustling legs, and carried, bent forward, the sack to the basement, after the hired man. The hired man had turned on the light in the basement, and broad and black, the coachman entered the light shaft of the basement stairs. The sound of the sack being emptied down in the basement confirmed my conjecture that the sack contained coal. The emptying of the coachman's sack made the same sound; besides, I followed the coachman and thus could verify with my own eyes that it was coal which fell dustily from the sacks in the wooden partition next to the furnace. The hired man turned to the basement door, folding the empty sack, went to the basement door and through the door, up the stairs, across the yard, past the kitchen steps; and the coachman followed the hired man, also folding his sack; outside there were voices and steps which suggested that the housekeeper and the boarders were going back into the house. The hired man showed up again with a full sack on his back, a sack he emptied over the partition and carried back empty and folded, meeting the coachman who was also carrying a new sack on his back, a new full sack which he, like the hired man, emptied, folded and carried back, meeting the hired man, who again carried a full sack on his back, a full sack that was emptied, folded, and taken back, when the coachman showed up again, a sack on his back whose contents he poured onto the coal heap over the partition, a sack

53

which was folded and taken away just like the sack of the hired man who now showed up with it again, and like the next sack of the coachman's and the next sack of the hired man's and all the following sacks of which I lost count. What I didn't understand, considering the large number of sacks and the size of the coal heap, was how all these sacks filled with coal had found room in the coach which hadn't even seemed fully loaded; and after I had gone back and forth several times between the coach and the coal heap in order to compare the spaces, this became even more incomprehensible. Had there been sacks on the top of the roof; the coachman whom I asked denied it; and what reason could he have to lie to me; also I would certainly have noticed them at the arrival, and, with a load of sacks behind him, the coachman's outline wouldn't have stood out as clearly above the coach as it had while the coach was coming nearer. During the meal, which the coachman ate on the free place to my left, I asked him again: don't you think, coachman, that the heap of coal in the basement is by far greater than the capacity of the coach, and how do you explain that; to which he answered without looking up from his spoon full of potatoes and beans: just illusion. Unsatisfied by his answer I turned to the hired man and asked him: didn't it strike you too, hired man, that the amount of coal in the basement is larger than could have found room in the coach; which he answered this way, chewing potatoes and beans in his mouth: in sacks tighter, heap more loosely, no wonder. But this explanation didn't satisfy me either, even though both the coachman's and the hired man's words may have contained a grain of truth; and even today, three days and three nights later, I haven't found an explanation for the unproportionately large difference between the space the coal could fill in the coach and the space it filled in the basement. Fighting hard against my sleepiness and my impulse to put the pencil down and give up these notes, I think back to the evening three days and three nights ago and go on describing this thinking back; and the fourth night is already beginning with supper finished and me having withdrawn from the boarders gathered in the hall; the fourth night after the evening when the coachman, after we had left the gathering in the hall for our rooms, followed the housekeeper who was carrying the coffee mugs into the kitchen to the sink, followed her into the kitchen and stayed there with her, which I could see from the shadows falling from the kitchen window onto the ground in the yard while I was leaning out of my window inhaling the night air. As I calculated, the shadows must be thrown by the bulb of the adjustable lamp in the middle of the kitchen, and considering the position of the shadows, the lamp must have been pulled down to chest height, probably to light up the floor which the housekeeper intended to scrub; I therefore distinctly saw the shadow of the coffeepot stick up over the shadow of the windowsill, and, to the side, about from the place where the housekeeper sat at meals, the shadow of the housekeeper bent over the table with arms stretched out and the shadow of the coffeepot. Now the coachman's shadow, rising from the back of the kitchen and growing beyond the shadow of the edge of the table on the same level as the shadow of the windowsill, appeared next to the housekeeper's shadow; the shadow of his arms reached into the shadow of the housekeeper's arm, and also the housekeeper's other arm joined the now swelling shadow of the arms, whereupon the shadow mass of the housekeeper's body came close to the shadow mass of the coachman's body and fused with it. Only the shadow of the housekeeper's raised hand holding the coffeepot stuck out from the shapeless, condensed joining of the bodies' shadows. The shadow of the coffeepot swayed back and forth, the shadow of the bodies also swayed back and forth; and now

55

and then the shadow of the heads in profile, sticking close together, rose above the clump of the bodies. After a violent side movement of the bodies, the shadow of the coffeepot broke free from the shadow of the hand and fell down; for a few seconds, the shadows of the bodies came apart; the housekeeper's body with the arching breast line leaned back on the table; the coachman's shadow opened and rose up high with wild gestures and as if flapping his wings, throwing off the bulk of his coat's shadow. After the coat shadow had slid off the shadow of the coachman's body, the shadow of the coachman's body thrust forward again, and the shadow of the housekeeper's body came to meet him with the shadows of the housekeeper's arms reaching into the shadow of the coachman's body, beyond and around it, and the shadows of the coachman's arms dug into the shadow of the housekeeper's body and around it. With jerky, jolting movements, the shadows of the bodies turned and edged farther toward the middle of the shadow of the windowsill and table edge; the shadows of the housekeeper's legs (she was lying on the table) rose with bent knees above the shadow of the coachman's body as it crept forward; and the shadow of the coachman on his knees rose above the shadow of the housekeeper's belly. The shadow of the coachman's hands delved into the shadow of the housekeeper's skirt; the shadow of the skirt slid back; and the shadow of the coachman's belly burrowed into the shadow of the housekeeper's bared thighs. The shadow of one of the coachman's arms bent toward the shadow of his lower body and pulled out a rodlike shadow which, in form and position, corresponded to his sexual organ; this questing shadow he thrust in the heavy, full shadow of the housekeeper's body, after the shadows of the housekeeper's legs had risen to the shadow of the coachman's shoulders. The shadow of the coachman's lower body rose and sank in an accelerating rhythm over the responsive, dancing shadow of the housekeeper's body while the shadows of their heads remained locked in profile. Finally, the shadow of the housekeeper's body reared up, and the shadow of the coachman's body threw itself with full force into the shadow of the housekeeper's body, whereupon the shadows of both bodies, fusing, broke down and stayed stretched out on the shadow of the table, rising and falling in heavy respiration. After a while, the coachman's shadow rose and moved away from the housekeeper's shadow, and the housekeeper's shadow also rose up; and from further movements of the shadows I gathered that both the coachman and the housekeeper left the table and went to the back of the kitchen where their doings were hidden from me. Shortly after they had gotten up from the table I heard the kitchen door open; then I saw the housekeeper and the coachman go down the kitchen steps and across the yard to the coach. I could not make out the coach in the dark; I could only conclude from the sounds that the coachman was getting the coach and the horse ready for the return trip; and sure enough, soon afterward, the shaft, the bridle, and the wheels began creaking, and the horse's steps clattered on the road, resounding further and further away, as did the rattling and squeaking and creaking of the coach, until it died down altogether in the silence of the night. And this too, the fact that the horse, after having pulled the load of coal for such a long way during most of the day, had to go back the same way the night following this same day, this made me wonder, so that I couldn't get to sleep that night, three days and almost four nights ago

57

CONVERSATION OF
THE THREE WAYFARERS

TRANSLATED FROM THE GERMAN BY

Rosemarie Waldrop

THEY were men who did nothing but walk walk walk. They were big, they were bearded, they wore leather caps and long raincoats, they called themselves Abel, Babel and Cabel, and while they walked they talked to each other. They walked and looked around and saw what there was to see, and they talked about it and about other things that had happened. When one was talking the two others kept still and listened or looked around and listened to something else, and when one of them had finished saying what he had to say, the second one spoke up, and then the third, and the others listened or thought about something else. They had stout boots for walking, but they carried only as much with them as would fit into the pockets of their clothes, as much as they could quickly lay their hands on and put away again. Since they looked alike they were taken for brothers by passersby, but they were not brothers at all, they were only men who walked walked walked, having met each other by chance, Abel and Babel, and then Abel, Babel and Cabel. Abel and Babel had met each other on the bridge, Babel, who had been coming toward Abel, turned round and joined company with Abel, and Cabel ran into them in the park and since then they walked walked walked everywhere together.

I believe this bridge is a new one, I have never seen it before, it must have been built overnight, a difficult job requiring long preparation and a great expenditure of effort. Pontoons were towed in and barges with planks, the pontoons were anchored, the planks set in place and lagged fast, after careful calculations and with the help of a selected workforce. Master-builder, engineers, workmen, members of the city administration knew months ahead about the bridge, when people were still calling to each other from the open banks. At that time rowboats traveled back and forth through the rapids, also a flat open ferry. Have often crossed on the ferry, the trip an interval of standing still and despite that of moving forward, on the blue water, under clouds and seagulls. The ferry engine puffed, vibrations came up through the deck into the soles of your shoes, up your legs, into the body, as in regular quick walking. The ferryman's face was covered with shining white stubble, his skin was darkly tanned and covered with lines and furrows. He lived in a shack over there on the bank, near the pile to which the ferry lay tied up. During the crossings I talked with him, his words were unclear because he always had a pipe held between his teeth, a short sturdy pipe wound with wire and insulating tape. In our most recent conversation he seemed not to have known about the projected bridge. If I understood him correctly he foresaw a long future for himself on his pounding, wave-cleaving ferry, in the blue air, in wind and in rain, and many planks had gone into putting the ferry together, and many nights in his shack, with the view through the window of the pile with the tautly stretched hawser. It is possible that he had built the ferry himself in his early years, not alone, but with the help of other boatbuilders, perhaps he was only a helper, in any case he knew how many planks had gone into putting the ferry together, and how many ribs and bolts had been needed for its completion. It had often been repaired and tarred since then, nonetheless water steadily leaked in, every morning he had to pump out. When the tower clock on the castle struck out another full hour he traveled from the bank where his shack lay across to the other bank, no matter whether any ferry passengers had come aboard or not, or whether any passengers were waiting on the other side. He came back the same way from the other bank and if people came running from afar he did not wait and the people over there could shout and whistle as much as they liked, he came back only when the hour had run out again.

The bridge has existed for a long time. I was riding one time in a black lacquered, redly upholstered coach over the bridge and next to me sat my bride and vomited on her white dress because the bridge swayed on the pontoons and the sections of the roadway rose and fell. The coachman in front of us up on the driver's seat just lifted his whip, which was decorated with a white ribbon, and the horse lost his footing, buckled at the knees and remained prostrate in a confusion of harness. From the impact of the vehicle behind us, in which my bride's parents were sitting, we were thrown forward, a bursting of wood could be heard, a neighing, a thunder of hooves, and the other horse, which had torn itself loose, broke into a gallop between the lines of autos, a gray horse speckled all over with red, like the bridal veil that was fluttering out of the window. One of the shafts of the coach behind us had punched through our conveyance and its splintered point stuck out through the upholstery. The coachman ran after the runaway horse, his woolen waterproof flapping, swinging his whip, and the occupants of the automobiles that had come to a stop stuck out their heads. The fallen horse lay on his side, motionless, his legs stuck out stiffly from him, except for the broken foreleg, over the bloody bone-stump of which our coachman bent down. With eyes obliquely straining the

63

horse looked up at him, his head patiently leaned on the
shaft, his nostrils and ears trembling, and wavy lines and
whorls shimmering through the dark brown skin about the
forehead, eyes and nose. The roadway rocked, the waves
rose high, the wind whistled and, under the weight of the
stalled traffic and the people who had rushed up to see, the
bridge sank. Policemen and firefighters arrived, the wail of
the sirens audible from a distance, brought lines with them,
cranes, stretchers and tools, and men in helmets and rubber
coats knelt about the horse, freed it from the traces, tied it
fast under the arm of the crane on the wrecker and the
horse let it all be done to him, softly snuffling, a little foam
at his mouth, and officials with whistles and brusque mo-
tionings with their white gloves got the traffic moving
again. As the horse under the derrick was being slowly
swung onto the floor of the truck he turned his head in
astonishment toward the coachman, and likely saw him for
the last time, and while the horse, lying on his side, was
being tied down, police came this way from the park with
the other, recaptured horse, which reared and the policemen hung onto him by his bridle, their legs dangling high.
The shaft was pulled out of the back wall of our coach, we
got in with my bride's parents, I forced myself in between
them, took my bride on my lap, both coachmen harnessed
the redly speckled horse between the shafts, climbed up
onto the seat, held the reins pulled taut, and the coach in
which we had been riding was hitched to the back of a
firetruck, and thus everything was able to get rolling again,
on the floating bridge, in the sea wind, under the screaming gulls. The police car led the procession, then came the
red truck with the fallen horse and the men on either side,
followed by the empty coach being towed, jolting along
and swinging this way and that, and finally our vehicle,
with two coachmen on the driver's seat, close together, in
light gray cloaks, the collars thrown back wide over their

shoulders, light gray top hats on their heads, with feather plumes on them, I believe, and while I could see nothing that was going on because my bride's veil lay over my face, we flew back in the coach with a jerk, and then it became evident that the horse, after it had left the bridge, snorting and striking sparks from the cobbles, had overtaken the men on the wrecker, and the police car, which was now moving along beside us, again sounded its siren as it proceeded. I held my bride wrapped in my arms, at my right her father leaned far out of the window, and her mother at the left leaned still farther out, yet whereas the father shouted stop, the mother screamed for us to go faster, her hat, garnished with flowers and lace, had fallen from her head, she threw herself backward and forward, her face contorted in a wild joy, with shrill shouts she spurred the horse on, and the vehicles in front of us scattered to one side, pedestrians flew from the sidewalk into the park, where a brass band was making music, and not until we· got to the square, which we circled several times, did we come to a halt, after two police cars, pressing in from right and left, got the horse squeezed in between them, and this happened in front of the entrance to the hotel, where the room for the wedding night had been engaged, the porter was already standing there, ready to receive us.

Yesterday I made another trip on the ferry, and the ferryman told me about his sons, he had six sons, and this morning, as I traveled across, he told me about three of them, this evening, as I came back, he told me about the three others. The first son was small and round, I don't know whether he was the oldest, in any case he was the first to be mentioned. He had red cheeks and red hair, short fat arms and puffy hands. He held his mouth open, he had very small sharp teeth and a pointed nose, his nose was turned up and when it rained, it rained into all the openings in his face. The second son was long and thin, his eyes lay deep in their sockets, his skull was bald, his cheeks sunken in. He had only one arm, the other had been eaten away by gangrene. But with his remaining hand he could do lots of things better than many with two hands, playing skat and perhaps playing the piano, too. The third son was built like a giant, he had a coarse moustache and bristly hair, his chest was tattooed and could, when he expanded it, break an iron chain. His arms were full of scars, for he stuck needles and knives through them, and his gullet and the pit of his stomach were all beat up by swords that he stuck into them and drew out. The fourth son, according to the description, seemed to be older than the ferryman himself, which could be explained by the fact that he was a stepson whom his mother had brought along into her marriage. This son had no teeth and was able to move around only with difficulty, on crutches. When he uttered any words at all, he stammered, and nobody had the patience to hear him out. However, he always let everybody know he was there by banging a crutch on the table, and when he had been locked in the attic he banged on the floor. The fifth son was everyone's favorite. He was stout, too, much fatter than the first son. He was so fat he could scarcely move, he passed the time on the sofa, on the floor, in bed, where big pillows lay ready for him everywhere. The ferryman's eyes filled with tears when he talked about this son. He said, if I didn't misunderstand him, that he always brought him something every day when he came home from work. At that time he was still living with his family in a bigger house on the knoll beyond the bank, where the telegraph office now stands. He came home with a fish, a cherry, a snail, a cauliflower, always with something different, which he held behind his back as he came in, while the son, hearing his steps outside, impatiently wanted to know what he had brought home with him today. What did you bring me today, what have you got nice for me today, cried the ferryman in weepy mimicry, and it was one of those rare moments when he took the pipe out of his mouth. On tiptoes the ferryman would approach the place where his son was lying, meanwhile urging him to guess, and because the son always guessed wrong, the surprise was always great, and then with his own hands the ferryman would prepare the gift on the stove or the kitchen table and serve it to his son on his special plate, on the center of which was painted a dwarf with a pointed red cap. Naturally this dainty was only something special, for the mother had already cooked and spiced the main meal, yet before they all went in to eat they looked in on the bedridden son, with nods of their heads and encouraging laughs, as he ate up his hors d'oeuvre. Only the sixth son did not look on, he often had to be restrained by force by the other brothers, because he wanted to attack the fat one with a knife. The sixth son's face was of great beauty, though eaten away by the pox. He had long silky black hair that hung down to his shoulders. He wore a golden ring in his left ear and on his fingers a couple of cheap rings. He cared nothing about his clothes, they hung on his body in rags, and everywhere the yellow skin shone through. This son never slept in the house, but in a box outside in the yard which he had surrounded with barbed wire. He was big, too, but walked bent over and shambling, barefoot, or in raggedy foot-wrappings. The ferryman named names for me, too, perhaps, they were the names of his sons, and so the first was called Jam, the second Jem, the third Jim, the fourth Jom, the fifth Jum, the sixth Jym.

The bridge has been there a long time, we once rode over the bridge on the way to the registry office, a woman and

I. She had come up to my place of an afternoon, I didn't recognize her again at first, had also forgotten her name, and I led her into the kitchen, her belly was sticking out. You've grown stout, I said, trying to place her, and her only answer was to smile. She sat down, sat in front of me with her legs spraddled out, held up her belly for me to see, and confidently smiled. She took hold of my hand and laid it on her belly and I felt the child moving. All the questions I asked she answered with puckerings of her lips and her belly was her only answer. I had forgotten the hours when, as she later explained to me, we had embraced in the hall to the staircase of the Academy of Science behind the guard's little cubby, under the plaster copy of the Nike of Samothrace. Imperishable hours, payment for which I was now on the way to make good before the mayor's legal counsel, and we walked into a wood-paneled room in front of a wooden rail, behind us two guards hired as witnesses, and the official knocked three times on a hollow box and looked at my future spouse's pregnant belly, and compelled us to get down on our knees on a wooden footstool, and we held fast to the wooden rail, and he read his formulas, which ticked away, hollow-sounding, in the wooden chamber, and then we wrote down our names, for all eternity, in a thick book that he held out to us.

There, I think, the ferryman just rode by, in the last car of the trolley, at the brake-wheel, he held the wheel in his hands and turned it this way and that, surely it was he standing there in the crowd, only he had such a broad-rimmed hat, so beaten up by sun and rain, only he held his short thick pipe so firmly in his mouth. After the ferry had been taken away from him, he had to find a steering wheel on the streetcars, and so he stood there, legs spread apart, his back turned toward the direction the car was traveling, and saw the street flowing away before him, with automobiles pressing on in the foam of the wake, with thick lines of swimmers left and right in the mist and the waves. I visited him once when he was still living in the house on the knoll on the bank, when, as you recall, there used to be foliage, fishermen's houses, barns and stables on the hills, with farms and pasturelands, also a wood. At that time smallholders lived over there, had goats, chickens, pigs, and as children we often went over there Sundays on the ferry and cut ourselves rods from the hazel bushes, while our parents, mother with her parasol, father with his bamboo cane, walked along the paths through the fields. Although the bank over there belonged to the city, we were out in the country, hay-wagons came from the fields and cows grazed in a meadow, slowly coming this way side by side, always turned in the direction of sunset, of an evening lining up in a common movement, parallel to one another. I thought to myself about it, why they always kept the same direction, and I concluded that it was governed by a natural economy, whereby they grazed the whole breadth of the field in a row, missing not a single tuft, and when they had reached the outermost edge of the field the grass behind them had grown up again, and the ferryman, who owned the cows, drove them back to a fresh start, which for the cows was only a continuation of the same. They chewed the grass into themselves with rolling mouths, meanwhile staring straight ahead with their dark eyes, made their tails hit their flanks, from time to time lifted their tails stiffly, broadly braced out their legs, and let steaming, golden-colored water stream out of them, let spicy brown excrements plop down in broad flaps, chewed, lay down, chewed some more, got up again, bent their heads deep into the grass, seized it with their tongues, ripped it off, shoved it into their mouths, chewed and transformed the green brew into white milk, which the ferryman's wife

milked from their udders, while the cows stood still, chewing, their heads lifted, staring off over the water, sometimes
bawling deep out of their throats. During this procedure
we looked on and perhaps she let us take hold the teats and
press out a stream, I do not clearly remember, it is so long
ago. In any case we followed her, a couple of children from
the city, into the house, we carried the pail for her and in
the kitchen were allowed to drink out of wooden beakers
which she dipped into the pail. The rim of the beaker felt
thick on the lower lip and the milk came warm and fat
into the mouth and the taste of grass. On the wall hung a
white clock, with large ornamented numbers and hands,
with a pendulum swinging this way and that and two chains
with weights in the form of pine cones. The ferryman sat
at the table and had spread out a newspaper in front of him,
he read half aloud and sucked on his pipe. His wife looked
at us, how we were drinking the milk, and wiped her hands
on her apron. The ferryman paid no attention to us and
when he saw us on the ferry he pretended not to recognize
us however much we asked him how his cows were and
about the cement dwarf standing in his garden.

My father goes into that white house there, the one that
takes up the whole side of the street. I saw him clearly, it
was my father, I can show you a picture of him. You can
see him here in the photo, the picture goes back to his early
years, he has changed very little, still has his smoothly
parted hair, still wears this tight-fitting suit with sloping
shoulders, these pointed, light-yellow shoes with gray
spats. Perhaps he is still living in this house, or has his business here. A huge building, the outside wall covered with
slabs of white stone, down below the reception hall and
salesrooms, over the rows of offices, yet no sound from the
typewriters and adding machines comes through the walls

and double windows. From the staircase of the uppermost story he opens the door of his apartment, a sound recognized by the children out back in their rooms, they hear him clearing his throat, they hear the door closing shut. It is dark in the vestibule, only place where a little light comes through is the glass door to the corridor. Umbrella stands beside the mirror, on the mirror dragons or angels, a low table with a silver salver and in the shadow of the wall the row of things hung up, everything likely to form youthful memories. Behind the glass door a long corridor, somewhere on a ramification of it my room, a long narrow room with a target for darts on the door. Stood there in the back part of the room and threw darts into the round cork plate, with red and blue circles painted on it, and the door opened once when I had forgotten to bolt it and the dart had already been thrown and hit my father in the middle of the forehead, stuck there, with its red tail-feathers, in the white forehead, and he still holding fast to the doorknob.

It is a new house, here before were located the port authority buildings, red brick ones with arched gates leading to courtyards, gates on which flags were hung on holidays on slanting flagstaffs. On the outer quay the tracks for the big traveling cranes are still to be seen, and where dark asphalt border-strips have been laid into the pavement once ran the tracks for the freight cars, which were pulled by the little hissing locomotive with a tapering red breastplate and a bell that rang during the trip and when it was winter smoke hung long in the air in thick white balls. Here stood the warehouses with sliding iron doors, in the warehouse stalls boxes, sacks, barrels were stacked up, here, too, out on the cobbled pavement lay cargo which had been lifted out of the ships, arranged according to category, in its packing, with stamps, numbers, trademarks, names of foreign countries and harbors. What had not been stowed away remained outside at night, roped up and covered with green tarpaulins, and a couple of watchmen walked up and down the sparsely lighted quayside with a revolver holster at their belts, perhaps with a dog, too, which they led on a leash. One of the ferryman's sons worked here, as a packer, in the winter, in the summer he went to the booths at the fair, there he stood, Jim, his bristly head bent far back, on a platform, surrounded by colorful pictures in which you could see snakes and lions, buffalo and Indians, uniformed apes, palm trees, cannibals and pirate ships. Into his gaping mouth he thrust the broad shining sword, deep into the gullet, down through his throat, into his stomach, until only the pommel was showing and after he had spread his arms out sideways slowly he drew it out again and the spittle and gastric juices dripped from the blade. And when things were in full swing at the docks and more help was needed, Jem could be seen there, too, called in by Jim, and he stuck a steel hook into a crate, swung it to him and with his one hand did more work with draw-chains and nets than many another with two hands. However, farther along everything is still the way it used to be, customs house, shipping offices, freighters, and despite the rolling iron-tired cartwheels, despite the pounding feet, the nets and the chains slid over the ground, despite the rust, the spilled oil and the hot water from the locomotive, grass is growing everywhere between the stones, at the base of the warehouses, on the cemented slopes the grass stands high, with stinging nettles and thistles, soon the grass will overgrow the quay, the stones will be broken to bits sprung apart by the grass, bushes will grow out of building walls, roots will take hold in every joint, cracks will split open in the walls and everywhere seeds blown in by the wind will, consuming themselves, get a fasthold in the sand-dust, a wilderness will arise from the rubble and years later we shall crawl about here through the under-growth, discover remains of buildings, rusted tracks among roots and mosses, and within the ruins everything will be thickly hung with spider webs, even now the spiders are at work, spinning spinning, in the corners of the warehouses, over there the window openings with iron bars on them are full of thick gray webs which swing in the draft, the panes broken, grass in the loam-dust in the cracks of the window frames, in the bird droppings, flocks of birds will nest here, wild dogs, wild cats will roam through the bushes.

At night everything here is forsaken, not even a watchman to be seen. On such a night I carried something down here, from the old city, I came running along the alleyway bent forward, puffing, because what I was carrying was the essence of seven years of prejudice, habit and fallacy, which had suddenly fallen into my lap, I had it all, every bit to myself, could no longer share it out and shove it off onto someone else, nor could I throw it away, either, for it was still my property, it still belonged to my seven fat years, and I lugged it here down the steep alleyway, down to the quay, on the double, and for the occasion I came up with all sorts of art things, so as to get away from stuff that for a moment had struck me as meaningful, I let out cries of negation and struck out with my fist, I breathed out steam and let salty water stream out of me, each step was a trampling, each arm movement an annihilation of doubts of wonderful forcefulness, in that my knuckles became bloody because of it, and no one here crossed my path, it was all emptiness among the formless heaps in their pack-ing, the crates, the trestles and hawsers, untrammeled I could rage about with my property, tinkling and with pointed red breast, until, hours later, I climbed up the alley again, past the monument up there, the eagle with the outspread wings, a hare in his claws, opened the house gate through which I had left, climbed up the stairs, five stories, a steep spiral in crudely slapped-together walls, a stone shell all spotty and scraped away to nothing, holes bored into the plaster by poking fingers made bigger, at the stair-edges a painted white ornamentation worn out by use and washing, and arrived at the door at the top of the stairs. I could still take it, I could still carry a load and with it rush about at great speed, so much I had proved to myself, and now I stood still, below the stair-landing, leaned against the curve of the wall, the right foot two steps below the left foot, and before me saw the light-blue door, with a slot for letters, a brass doorbell, the kind turned with a winged key, a dark-blue nameplate with white letters. I took in these details so exactly because in each of them I was still recognizing the past I longed for, I stood still, listened hard, was aware of a seething stillness, in it a splashing and dripping. Behind the door, the key to which I still carried in my pocket, I heard nothing, and now I imagined as in setting a stage the objects and spaces behind the door, the doormat, and on along the runner, on to the walls with the burlap pasted on them, walls on which hung pictures of bulls, suns, lightnings and fire-spewing mountains, past the clothes-hangers with pieces of clothing, her fluffy overcoat, her raincoat, her kerchief, her checkered sports cap, the boots under it, as far as the door leading to the adjoining room. I cross the big room quickly, it was dark by now, she lay behind in the bedroom, under the sloping window, through which on a clear night the moon and the famous constellations were to be seen. And now he was looking out with her from the bed through the high window, or he twisted himself and looked at her, saw the strands of black hair spread out on the pillow, saw her mouth, her nipples outlined blackly on the fair skin. In the mirror on the back wall lay pooled the inverse image of the big anteroom, in which the recessed windows in the wall stood flung open, and through them came the same sounds from the street that I heard in muffled version from my vantage point. By the apartment door on the landing was a box that once had served for storing firewood, it was long empty now, I lifted the cover and crept into the box, inside which there was a smell of moldering bark. And I still carried everything with me into the box, my arms full of riches, and nested myself down in the wood-dust, lay there awake until it became lighter, then climbed out again, again took up my post in the winding stairs, leaning on a pilaster, left foot two steps below the right foot, ready with a nimble turn to resume my course about the arena. Coming up from the streets could be heard the sounds of milk bottles rattling and the banging of garbage pails being emptied into garbage trucks, and down below in the stairwell doors opened and slammed shut, and children skipped down the steps on the way to school. Steps hesitantly approached, came to a halt here and there, followed by the sound of mail slots opening and falling shut, whereupon slowly I went down the stairs and as he with the mailbag came by I looked the other way and tied my shoelace. Up above he threw a letter into the slot then, breathing heavily, descended, throwing himself from step to step, a heavy older man, and now I looked him in the eye, we recognized each other, he went past, smelling of sour leather, fell step by step into the depths, and soundlessly I climbed up again, and stood just below the landing and heard how the letter was being picked up within, heard her voice and his voice, then through the ventilator in the wall next to the door I heard how she lit the gas stove, put coffee on, set cups out on the table and over it all lay seething silence. Over there the man in the black suit, with the stiff black hat and the black sunglasses, he could be the one I had seen her with coming out of the house that time, he was dressed differently then, wore brown Manchester pants, a brightly checkered shirt, a checked cap. I stood concealed in the entrance arch across the way from them in order to avail myself of the drama of it, as they went close by me arm in arm, and I followed them, waited behind the eagle statue, and when they had gone up and away I sneaked after them, I showed how tenacious I was, I don't know how many days and nights, no end of it in sight, it had been merely a beginning, I had hardly dared face up to the first scene of the play. There I stood, before I ended up that time in quayside precincts, having pressed forward into the middle of the room upon returning from a journey, having already seen his topcoat, his jacket outside in the clothes closet, and heard his voice, which grew louder when I went in, and now I saw him, comfortably leaned back on the low sofa in shirtsleeves, barefoot, and she on a cushion on the floor in front of him, her arms on his knees, her face turned toward me, white as the walls of the room, and in this second the plunge downward began, I fell and fell, and the room, the house, everything fell with me until the stage of weightlessness had been reached, whereupon I flew this way and that, out and away and down, in a single swoop down five stories, along the street, to the beautiful hard flat surfaces and sharp-edged posts, amid which everything was fixed and steady and could reverberate on me, and then again up and into the box and mornings before the gas flame, the clinking of coffee cups, the wordless voices and down into hiding in the gateways and courtyards, up there between those baked-together walls, there where the street runs into the square and the green feathers of the bird materialize, the bird that is perhaps no eagle at all but a parrot, and there where I crept up the stairs to skulk at the threshold. So it was, as countless times before I come up the familiar staircase, dressed in black after my father's funeral, hold the key ready in my hand and hear, before I stick it into the keyhole, voices and sounds from within which create the impression that I am in a strange domicile. Hesitantly I open the door, again I recognize the clothes closet, but the articles of clothing in it are strange to me, no traces of my earlier presence are to be discovered. The laughter of the woman within dies away, by the same token the man's laughter becomes all the louder, and I walked from the entrance hall into the living room in which I have lived for years, but which now harbors strangers. The eyes which greet me stare at me as if I were an intruder, carried by momentum I advance to the middle of the room, still bent on taking possession of it, on lying down there on the low red sofa, on taking off my shoes, stretching out after the journey, for the woman still seems familiar to me, her face, her hair, her morning coat I have often seen, but already I am beginning to wonder, perhaps it's her sister, a distant relative, someone only remotely like her, besides her face before had more color, now it melts into the whiteness of the wall, the features no longer are recognizable, and I raise my finger, want to say something, explain my presence, but I cannot get the words out. On the other hand the man speaks right up to the unbidden guest, he takes the glass standing on the table by the flask and drinks to me, the woman draws nearer to the sofa and holds fast to the recumbent man's naked foot. And while the strength which has been impelling me forward suddenly reverses itself and with a rapidity that steadily increases pulls me downward, I still stand balanced on the flatness of the floor and thus press the flying floor with me into the depths, I am forced to recognize that my visit has been a mistake, that perhaps I did indeed live here once, that perhaps, too, the period of seven years which floats before me has a certain validity, but that thereafter, however, intervals followed which I lost out of sight and reckoning and despite a dim and distant remembrance renewed, nothing any longer fits in with my old ideas. At this moment I wanted to prevail over time become unrecognizable, I continued to keep my forefinger upraised in order to explain this lost time away as a nullity, yet in the swiftness of my downward plunge any movement backward was impossible, it was only evident that what lay behind me could never be reached again, that nothing was known of me any longer in this room, and the man still nodded at me, glass at his mouth, and the woman's snowy face completely disintegrated.

Once I went through a city, a wandering that lasted for several days and nights. I had stepped out of a bus after the conductor had asked me several times what my destination was and finally, after I could not name it, he had kicked me out. I came through districts where there were docks and shipyards, and when, at a crossing, I ran into the same policeman who had seen me before, he stopped me and asked for my papers. I had them with me, also knew who I was, although that meant nothing to me. As yet I had not forgotten my own name, though I had forgotten what I was doing here and what city it was that I was in. Since my papers were in order I was allowed to go my way. I spent the first night in a room over a bar, the floor sloped sharply, everything was tipped, in bed I first lay with my head toward the foot, then changed my position, and until morning grayed I heard the banging and bawling from below. A washbasin stood on a three-legged stool, the door of the little closet in the corner was wedged shut with a piece of folded newspaper, a bulb with a green glass shade hung down from the ceiling, and beyond the window between fireproof walls a section of a river could be seen, now and then a tug, a launch. The room had an extraordinary immediacy and tangibility, in the morning I knew every bit of grain in the worn wooden floorboards, every bit of the flowered wallpaper, with its grease spots, finger-prints, nails and torn places, it was as if I had spent a life-time here. On the evening of the next day a couple of large figures walked close by me, right and left, I only felt them, did not see them. Where I spent the second night I do not know, perhaps I slept somewhere on the steps of a quayside landing, I remember the yellow water below me, and an iron ring against which I leaned, and the clatter of a motor-boat going by. Not until the evening of the third day had my name completely vanished from memory, I took out my papers, read the personal details inscribed on them, they meant nothing to me. When I got tired I lay down where I was, near the water on a smoothly rolled stretch of street, with wet places, splatters of spit, horse droppings. Lay there and was awake, felt fine, yet far away, saw myself from a distance lying there, did not budge. A couple of men came along and bent over me, their hands were blackened with oil, they wore dark-blue overalls, blue peaked caps with a shipping company badge. When they said they had a good mind to throw me into the water I did not stir, I knew they were testing me. They lifted me up, carried me to the edge of the quay, swung me about a few times and I let it all happen to me. Then they laid me down very close to the edge of the wall and went away. When I turned my face sideways I saw the water against the squared stone blocks, with refuse that had floated there, bits of wood, tin cans, sodden paper, a shoe without a sole, orange peels, foam.

Our footsteps grind in the gravel. A thickly populated city, with stony towers among the trees. The inhabitants here are prostrate, obliterated, soon even the nameplates on their houses will no longer be decipherable. Fresh wreaths, a new stone, still damp at its base. During her last hours I sat by my mother in her bed, in a room painted with shiny white enamel, and at the other side sat my father. She could no longer talk, she showed me what she wanted on a little pad. She indicated to us that we were to put our arms about her shoulders and then she leaned on us and it eased her breathing. She pointed to the pad, I handed it to her, and she wrote it would be nice now to have a cup of coffee. I rang, the servant appeared, we got the coffee. All her life my mother had cleaned other people's apartments and washed their laundry, an old servant's wish for a cup of coffee was a wish for the Sunday day of rest. She had scolded me, she had hit me, years on end, she had punished me with a belt, and she had screamed when my father had come home drunk and my father had beaten me until one day I threw him against the fireplace and the fireplace, with its white tiles, had collapsed, smoking, and Sundays we had drunk coffee in the kitchen. When she had emptied her cup I saw that she was holding my father's hand, they were both staring into space, my father and my mother, holding each other's hand, and my arm lay about their shoulders and we were the model of a family. She asked for her writing materials and wrote something with a shaky hand that I was able to spell out only later on. Then she became restless, scarcely had we helped her to get up out of bed than she let go her waters. I led her to the bed, looked for the pot, but did not know how I was to set her on it, and doing all this to me it was as if she were going to bear a child, as if it were her amniotic fluid that was warmly streaming over me, and so she died, lying backward over the edge of the bed, her legs spraddled out wide.

Here they lie in layers, among fish fossils, giant horsetails, ammonites, saurian bones and tin toys. Our steps crunch in the gravel of the paths. The ferryman once said to me, you can never really know who your father is and who is the father of your son. He told me about Jym. In later years this fellow had begun to wash himself, have his hair cut short, it was still long, but not so long that it hung matted over his shoulders, and his clothes were still far from conservative, he wore narrow trousers with black-and-white stripes, red silk vests, violet or blue jackets, shirts trimmed with lace. How he had managed to become rich remains a mystery, in any case he soon withdrew to a country house at the edge of the city, had servants and two cars, a mistress with blond corkscrew curls and a sunken mouth, and besides these a gardener, a saddle-horse, a groom and a yacht, which was tied up at a landing at the lower boundary of the lakeside property. Many a time at night the ferryman came with his skiff through a canal to the lake, lay there in the darkness and saw how the windows in the big house were festively lit, how the headlights of arriving cars swept through the park, how the guests went up the stairs to the open glass doors, and heard the music and the laughter. Once, in the summertime, a party of guests came running down to the shore, many threw off their clothes, others jumped into the water with their clothes on, and some of them swam out, one of them coming toward him. The ferryman sat still in his boat and saw how the head in the water was drawing nearer, with the mouth making soft blowing sounds. The swimmer came up to the side of the boat, the ferryman already could see the whites of his eyes shining, and the swimmer's hands stretched out, and the body came after them, and Jym was standing in the boat, bolt upright, naked, dripping. He stood there for some seconds, or minutes, the ferryman did not tell me just how long, then he again dived into the water, head first, swam back to the shore.

And when I hear our footsteps in the gravel of the walks,

here in this stillness behind the walls, then the other thing comes back to me, the thing that never had an end, and there I am, still lying in the sand, in front of an open barn, and am able to creep for a way along barbed wire, in a narrowly enclosed place overgrown with trees. There is no getting out when I am there, I can forget it all only for a time, by telling myself that I am awake, I am still alive, but then it comes back again, then it is all as before, and I torture myself with thinking about how it is going to happen, with the rope, the ax or by shooting, and again I crawl along the barbed-wire entanglement, and then back to the barn, and then I debate with myself about how I still might be able to escape, I imagine a feigned suicide, in which I cut the arteries in my wrist, smear myself with blood, and then I see them coming, perhaps they bury me on the spot, but perhaps they might tickle me and then I would have to laugh and I would be given the coup de grace. And if I am buried alive how shall I get out of the ground, many hundredweight of earth over me, my mouth full of earth. I could climb up a tree and then get away by swinging from tree to tree, but they are standing under every tree, they are laughing already, sooner or later I shall fall down into their arms. The trees are there to camouflage this area, there is a thick square of them and outside lies open field. I hear our steps in the gravel, I am awake, I think of the field, it lies clearly before me, I see each blade of grass on it, each flower, with the humming insects, I smell the earthy smell, I must have reached this field at some time or other, otherwise how could I see it so clearly, how could I, otherwise, be walking among you, how could I hear this gravel crunching if I were still lying there on the sand in front of the barn, at the barbed-wire barrier. Or do they have me already in their rifle-sights, are they letting me thrash about for a joke, and then I forget it all again for a time, thinking of this field right here and this gravel walk.

There they come, beyond the double gate, in their black, smoothly polished conveyance, they wear top hats, they sit up stiff and straight, they are hung with gold and silver, the driver glued to the steering wheel, the escort on ahead on motorcycles, in shiny black leather, and the onlookers stand pressed close together at the curbs. Now they come to a stop before the double gates. They get out, small, corpulent people with the fat force-fed faces of babies, the two smallest carrying a wreath behind which they all but disappear from view, they lay it down before the bowl at the gate, the bowl in which the eternal light burns, they take off their top hats, and the ones wearing uniforms salute with their hands at the peaks of their caps, and the women hold their hands folded on their stomachs, and the children gape open-mouthed, and now one of the little ones in front of the place where the light is burning begins to speak, he works his mouth yet his words cannot be heard. He pulls down his mouth with its thick pouty lips, his fat little cheeks begin to quiver, his eyes squeeze together, the veins in his neck swell. And all stare at the little flame, the little flame is reflected in the pupils of all eyes. What is he talking about with words that are not to be heard, he is talking about a game of skat at the regulars' table in the barroom or about the catch of fish last weekend, he is talking about the new suit he has ordered at the tailor's or about his son's bad school report, he is talking about his wife's false teeth or about the lamp that stands on his desk, he is talking about his daughter's illegitimate child, about the sausages he wanted for supper or about the weather that is beautiful today. It is not to be divined, what he says, and again he puts the tall hat on his round infant skull and the others do the same as he, and the hands fall away from the cap peaks, and everyone does aboutface and goes back to the waiting vehicles, the doors of which the drivers are holding open. What are the bystanders screaming, what are they shouting about, why are they throwing their hats in the air. The little fat ones pay no heed, they climb up onto their cushions, the leathery soldiers sit on their bikes in a knightly way, there is a rattle and roaring, then they drive away, leaving the onlookers in a cloud of blue gas.

The littlest one there, in the last car, is Jam, I recognize him now by his description, even though he has lost his red hair, but the gapy mouth, the holes in the puggy nose, the fat fingers are the same. The ferryman told me that he is in the civil service and has gone far, even back in school he was always the best, by squealing on his classmates to the teacher and no one dared beat him up because the teacher was on his side. Although they all hated him, most of them did his bidding, did his homework for him, carried his books for him, just so he would put a good word in for them. One of them who made no bones about being against him was kicked out of the school, for according to the story Jam caught him masturbating in the toilets and to prove it was able to point out the runny splotch on the wall. Later he destroyed others, too, by denouncing them as thieves or arsonists, and a teacher unwise enough to question his information, who indeed said out loud in the middle of a lecture that Jam didn't even know the rudiments of the subject matter, was dismissed from his post when Jam caught him making copulatory movements against one of the students. He also came out of the university with highest honors, after his informers had done his written work for him and he had been excused from the oral examinations, though not before the only dean who couldn't be bribed was laid low with a sudden stomach ailment. His uncontested rise took him to high posts, I believe to the position of director of education and head of all existing institutions of learning and culture, he served as model for many busts and medallions and his name was spoken with reverence.

And I know the little one who got into the first car, the one with the little silver stars and the cords on the peak of his cap, he was at the time when I stood before him still of lower rank, if well on the way to being promoted. We stood before him in a long row, our clothes we had removed outside in the corridor, and left on a wooden bench, we stood naked one behind the other, looking at the pimples and fleabites on the back of the man ahead, smelling the stink of sweaty feet and of armpit dampness, slowly we moved forward and the one in the lead was tapped, sounded, questioned, measured, weighed and shoved to one side. What is that, he asked me when it was my turn and pointed to the scar and the welt at my ribs in the region of the heart. A pistol shot, I said. He was sitting behind a writing table with a copyist at either side and they gnawed on their penholders, he still held his forefinger outstretched, then lifted it, bore into his nose-hole, turned it, drew it out again, wiped his nose with the back of his hand and stood up. He went around the table and stepped in front of me. He bent down to my scar and looked at it from as close as he could get. He touched it here and there with his forefinger, which was still damp from nasal mucus, and said the bullet was still in there to see, which I already knew. I know it is, I said. He looked at me from under his brows. His moustache, white today, at that time was still black, and he had bushy black eyebrows. I represent the army, he said. I know you do, I said. He thought of something to say, it was plain that he had made a false start and did not know where to go from there. Then his face suddenly lit up and he asked what battle it was I had got the slug. In the battle against myself, I said, I shot myself in the ribs. He sent an orderly to get a second-in-command to take over so he could deal with me undisturbed. He led me, naked as I was, across a courtyard where the women cooks of the establishment were doing calisthenics, and into a big room where a table was set for a banquet. All around on the walls hung coats-of-arms and crossed flags, and at the end of the hall rose a podium with a lectern. He ordered me to pull back the chairs from the table and arrange them in a serpentine row. Then, on hands and elbows, I was to creep in between the chairs as fast as I could, down the line, back and then down again. When I toppled over he struck me with the flat of his hand on my behind and cried up, up, get going, get going, and I hurried on, until I fell again. Then he ordered me to place the chairs at greater distances apart, and I had to jump from one chair to the next, from one end of the hall to the other and then back. Meanwhile figures in uniforms with trimmings in silver and gold had come in through side doors and were watching my exercises. Finally I had to put the chairs back and afterward go up on the podium. The figures sat down at the tables and the leader of the production stood beside the lectern, since he would have disappeared had he stood behind it. Gentlemen, he called out, and his voice was surprisingly powerful, with an expressive force that carried one away. All faces turned expectantly toward us, Gentlemen, you see before you an exemplary defender of our ideals. He tapped with the seal ring on his finger on the protuberance of flesh where the bullet had gone into my ribs, the while continuing his speech. The clinking that you hear, gentlemen, is a pistol slug which the same here shot into his chest with the intention of escaping from the service that confronts him. Subjected, however, to a certain calisthenics assignment, he showed abilities satisfying our strictest standards. Under my leadership he conquered himself. In spite of the bullet in his chest, with which he had wanted to put himself out of the way, he carried out what was asked of him, with glowing zeal he let himself be convinced that for him henceforth there was no evasion. Thus you see, gentlemen, a hero in the former coward and traitor, who will let himself willingly be detailed to the foremost ranks, and there every bit of courage, of endurance, of self-sacrifice, I have forgotten the rest of the speech. Thereafter I lived for years in hiding, in the woods, in sandpits, in an abandoned mine, earned my keep as a day laborer on remote farmsteads, always in flight from the police, until I found a ship where I was allowed to go aboard without papers and thus carried to other parts of the world. What do they amount to, these decades, I am now walking again along the same old streets, every stone, every tree known to me, there lies the exercise yard across which I was driven, the sentry boxes are still standing at the portals of the buildings, freshly painted but still shabby-looking, and the cannon to right and left still stick out their ridiculous barrels at us.

How quickly the mechanized column with its armored van- and rear-guard vanished in the flow of the street, and the people on the sidewalks still stare into the traffic long since closed in again, they are still hearing the sirens, the whistles that announced something was happening, but not a face behind the mirroring panes of glass rushing by had been recognizable. There they go now on their way, walk in through doors, come out through doors, alone, by twos, in groups, already we are coming again to streets earlier

traversed, the city is not so big that we could lose our way
in it, we always find the way again, it is almost as if we
belonged to this forward movement, as if we were at home
here, as if we ourselves had come here out of some hole
or other, as if there were someone here who was waiting
for us.

Here I had my hiding place, in the riverside district, here I
lay rolled together, smelled the dampness of the ground,
smelled the dampness in the air, under a pile of boards I
had made myself at home, and through the cracks I saw
the trains on the railroad embankment, I saw how the tug-
boats tipped down their funnels when they went under
the railroad bridge, how the smoke poured out blackly,
how the travelers leaned out of the windows and on the
way out looked back toward the city and coming in the
faces turned away from the city, and I saw the children
on the up-sloping scorched meadows, how they let their
paper dragons with long gaily colored tails climb into the
haze. From my scrap heap, my hole in the ground, where
I also lay out straight, I saw the insulators blooming on the
high-tension lines, the traffic signals at crossing points in
suburban streets, I saw the carts and the trucks which came
back in the gray of morning empty from the market hall,
and the heavy long-distance trucks with tied-down loads,
with the drivers high up on the driver's seat, the furniture
vans painted with winged horses, or with the emblems of
far-off cities, the cars that came in of a morning, at first one
at a time, hastily, an open ribbon of highway in front of
them, then ever more densely, sticking stubbornly to each
other, slowly moving forward under the electric wires, I
saw how the milkshops and the bakeshops opened their
doors, how the women bent out of the windows and waved
with their dust cloths, I saw the children with schoolbags

under their arms running to school, I heard the ringing of
the bell at the beginning of classes and the pneumatic drills
of the street-builders and the crashing of iron plates at the
shipyard, I heard the sirens of incoming and outgoing ships
from the harbor, and the buzzing of planes muffled by
clouds or standing out clearly in blue sky, I heard hammer
blows from the allotment gardens where a gardener was
fixing his fence, and from the woodworking shop I heard
the scream of the circular saw, I saw the garbage truck
coming, saw it lower its rump over the dumping spot and
empty its wet rushing contents, I saw the dump-pickers
rummaging around in the rubbish and I saw couples with
their arms linked on the way to the riverbank or to the
gravel piles, I saw how they stood still, I saw the changing
of the light over the fields, the shacks, the factories, over
the height with the newly built houses I saw rain and hail
fall, saw the vapor rising out of the ground, heard the
striking of hours from tower clocks.

On my travels I once lived on a beach. From my window,
or from the sand where I lay, I could see a narrow lagoon,
on which trees grew, they looked like palms, but were not
palms at all. Nor were there crocodiles and flamingoes, only
frogs and swarms of sandfleas. When my skin itched I went
into the still water and bathed. Once a week the ship came
to the jetty, tied up, then traveled farther along to the next
inhabited place, a day's journey away. Often I went aboard,
bought provisions and then again went to live on my beach,
disturbed by no one. I lived here and did nothing that left
a mark behind. At the most the minimum effort serving to
keep me fed had any point, catching a fish, picking mush-
rooms and berries in the woods, or lighting the fire for
cooking. Otherwise my thoughts were concerned with
nothing in particular, they posed no questions, constructed

no answers to fictitious problems. I slept when I was tired, I got up when I had slept long enough. I picked up stones, felt them out, let them fall again. I poked my finger into the sand, drew it out again, I chewed on a splinter of wood, or on a leaf and spat it out again. I saw a bird fly in the air and disappear behind trees, I saw clouds come in and sometimes ball together into thunderheads, I saw clear sky return again. No, it was on an island, I lived the summer there with a numerous family, and I waited for the day when the wife and child, brothers-in-law and sisters-in-law, nephews, female cousins and parents-in-law went back to the city and I could go to work in peace on the work for which I had been collecting material for years while we were moving from one apartment to another, the last always smaller than the one before. So the cutter left, fully loaded, when the vacation period was at an end, I heard the engine die away on the wind that had sprung up toward evening, and I climbed the hill to the log hut. I have often tried to explain to myself what it was that happened that night, and why I did not find the peace and composure I had anticipated, but fled in confusion from the island. The signs of a gathering storm were already unmistakable, the waves rolled in with white foam-crests, the clouds drove along low and broken in the sky, the trees swayed, all natural manifestations, and yet in it all a strange transformation could be felt. It still seemed possible to attain seclusion, to light the oil lamp on the table, get to work on the notes, yet every step I took toward a beginning led me farther from it, the papers lay ready, the lights were lit in all the rooms, but disturbances steadily increased. I stood in the middle of a flash-flood of movements and sounds, I heard each component part of this machinery, made up of water and foliage, boughs and grasses, of posts, bricks, wires and boards, I was able to discover holes and cracks in which the drafts of air got trapped, I heard this whimpering, whistling and hissing, this spraying, rattling, growling, scraping, scratching, squeaking and humming, this explosion of whistling and sucking, I went back and forth in the rooms and identified the origin of each sound until the agitation became so great that everything in it was indistinguishable, and when it made no difference how intensely I listened the other thing began, a quite different rushing and tearing, as if it might be something evoked by the air masses, a banging and rattling not created by the wind, a rumbling not caused by waves on the cliffs, a chattering and singing not possible among leaves and grasses. Now no more thoughts about work. Nights past when I had stepped over beds and gone out in front of the house I had been able to see the relationships among the aggregate of particulars, right off I drew logical inferences, now I had forgotten why it was that I had stayed on here, and all that was left was this pressure, this senselessness, and in this condition I landed outdoors again, perhaps because inside the house I felt myself caught in a trap, I had taken off my clothes, I stood outdoors in the seething rain and bellowed and flailed about with my arms, and ducked under the gigantic lashings of the trees, and this kept up the whole night long until finally, at the first shimmer of dawn, it died down and all that was left was a washed-outness, a feeling of physical exhaustion. What had happened already had become incomprehensible, only something of it had survived, and there were the trees and they stirred in the light spring wind and the grass whistled and the sea breathed in soft swells, and mechanically I packed my trunk, stowed away the papers, turned out the lamps, locked the house and went down to the rowboat lying on the pebbly shore. Going over to the mainland to the place where the steamers came in, all of it took place amid lassitude and a hollowed-out feeling like the feeling after a fever has passed, it was still hours before the steamer was to arrive, yet I was done with the island, I knew no more about the island and the time I had spent there, I tied up the boat, sat on the planks of the bridge in a stillness and emptiness, a uniform breathing, the sun rose in the sky, it became warm, over there the island flickered in the light, with the house on the hill among peaceful trees, and I sat in half-sleep leaned against a pile, and when the steamer whistle sounded from afar it was a signal of victory, and then the ship came up triumphantly, whitely shining, broad-breasted, snorting.

The time that the woman whose name I had forgotten came up to me one afternoon and held up her pregnant belly to me, I was living with someone else, and to this other one I returned after the proceedings in front of the wooden rail in the wooden city hall chamber had been completed. Within an hour I had left her, the one to whom I had sworn eternal fidelity, and who now went her way to bear my child, and I went back to the room where I had left the other one behind, and she sat in the same position in the armchair at the open window which she had taken upon my departure. The floor at her feet was wet from a shower of rain, her legs were wrapped in a blanket, her upper body was covered by a woolen jacket, her hands lay frozen on her knees, her head lay in the pillows, her eyes closed. When I stroked her hands her gaze flickered this way and that for a time before focusing on me. Her pupils were distended, she still did not recognize me, her eyes, the dark-red oval of the iris, the thick violet lashes, stared at me and now and again rolled up so high that only the bluish white eyeball could be seen. When I lowered myself onto her and touched her, shudders of cold passed over her skin, her body rose and sank back, and when she let me into her holding herself open for me with her hands, her face was twisted out of shape with horror. She screamed and clung hard to me, and then lay weeping and nights she awakened me, she sat upright in bed with muscles tensed and whispered, do you hear it do you hear it. What is it, I don't hear anything. How it's cracking and crunching. There in the middle of the room, there's someone cracking nuts and grinding his teeth. There's no one there, I said, and held her tightly. I'm lying on a white balcony, with a thin railing, she cried, and I said that it was an airy balcony and that I could see her from the open door and that it was light and that the balcony was securely fastened to the wall, yet she screamed that the white shutters in front of the balcony door were closed, that the balcony floor was thin as a piece of paper and that she dared not move, that she had to hold her breath so as not to tear the paper. The floor will hold you, I said, yet her face was distorted, her mouth gaped wide open, and then she saw a street, it was a bare street in a clean little city, at the beginning when she told me about this city everything seemed to be quiet and Sunday-like, the pavement was washed, the steps leading up to the doors shone with cleanliness, yet right away she began to tremble, she was alone in this street, in a short dress, a basket on her arm, and she began to run and to scream, why are you screaming, what are you really afraid of, and I could see nothing but the bare cobblestones, the gleaming steps and polished doorknobs, and she saw only her feet in white buckled shoes fleeing down the street. Her child shared this same terror and with him the terror was even more extravagant and his shrieking not to be appeased. We lived at the seashore, had arrived at the outskirts of the settlement as darkness was falling, amid dwarf pines and thorny bushes lay the little wooden houses, still empty and closed up at this time of the year. We walked against the sea wind, with the child, the baggage and in the bungalow it was cold and the beds were damp. The big suitcase, full of sheets and towels, was thickly soaked by

syrup that had run out of a broken bottle. I hung the
clammy blankets in front of the electric heater and she
carried the weeping child in her arms, she walked back
and forth with the child and rocked it, and I warmed milk
and then came the shrieking. She showed me the big scar
that ran across the child's chest and she said that the screaming came from the time of birth and that in this screaming
still lay the dread of suffocation and dying, for the child
had nearly suffocated at birth and that they had cut an
abscess out of his chest and it was because of this that he
had to scream, and she walked about with the child amid
the blankets hung on a line and redly lighted up and rocked
it in her arms and sang weepily in concert until the shrieking had worn itself out, then we lay down close together
under our overcoats and at dawn we saw a fly sitting on
the table, big as a man, it looked at us with eyes big as
plates, rotated its mandibles and bit into the wings of an
insect that it held in its claws, and the venation of the wings
crunched and burst like spun glass. And as always, when
she began to tremble at my side, when she screamed and
when tears rained from her eyes, I could only say, what's
the matter now, there's nothing there, I don't see anything,
and then she grabbed hold of me, and in moments of clarity
she cried, gray dwarf all covered with dust, gray mouse,
sowbug, you're going to die from the dust that's stuck your
eyes and mouth together, and then she spread herself open
to an imaginary lover and when she let me go into her she
was not aware of me, I hung over labyrinths and grottoes,
over coral reefs and sponge forests, and lost myself inside
her, and then she shoved me away from her, screamed
with excitement, and I rescued myself by retreating into
my indifference and self-control, I played the superior one,
it looked as if I were holding together while she was falling
apart, yet it was she who was living, even when she con-
sumed herself doing it, I only sat at the window in an

armchair and made my phone calls, and went over to city hall and the child in the belly of a strange woman poked me in the side when I pressed against her to seal our adventitious and immediately forgotten marriage with a kiss, and then again I sat in the armchair, and a cry came from the bed, of help me, they're coming now, they're coming now through the leaves, then I called back, it's nothing, it's nothing, be quiet, no one's there, and when the cry came they're grabbing me now and laughing at me and blowing in my face, I stood up and sat down beside her and put my arm about her and acted as though I could protect her, yet she was far away from me, I saw her not at all. And when she went away from me, not because she had met her great lover, but only because it happened that way, because the weather made for it, because the suitcases had fallen out of the cupboard against her, we quarreled on leaving over a broom, she wanted to take the broom along, I said I had bought the broom for the kitchen and for a while we both held onto the broom and tugged at it, and then she let me have it and I shoved it between my legs and took her bags and went out, and I flew on the broom about the house and experimentally flew for a way out the window, riding on the broom, and I saw her down below in the street, a suitcase in either hand, dressed in a red shawl, slung about her body and held by a cord, in gold-lacquered sandals, her hair falling down over her shoulders. Here, I will show you here an envelope with a black mourning border, here look, a strand of hair, color not recognizable, and here, she and I, arm in arm, a happy couple at the shore of a lake, her child with us, all three laughing, our black shadows behind us. The letter with the black border was received by my father from his father, when he informed him of the death of his wife, my father's mother, my father carried the letter about with him, with his mother's picture and the lock of his mother's hair, and the locks of hair lay in thin tissue paper, they still lie there, perhaps I have taken out the wrong one at times, or have got them mixed up, I have been carrying the letter with me a long time, since my father's death.

There you see Jom, at the entrance to the subway, the fourth ancient son of the ferryman, in rags, on crutches, babbling great sayings. After the household broke up he was driven out and had to start life on his own, it no longer did him any good when he pounded the floor with his stick or banged on the table, no one appeared, no mother any more brought him the pap he could swallow with his toothless mouth, he had to see how he could make out on his own, and he understood nothing. According to what the ferryman said it appeared that Jom lived somewhere among the packing paper and corrugated cardboard in the rubbish pile behind the railroad bridge, and if it is at all possible it must be there that he composes his odes, theme of which is that he knows nothing, that he understands nothing, that he cannot grasp just why he is where he is now or why he is at some other place, why he happens to run into this person or that one, why it is that it gets dark or light, or rains, or hails. If it can be so, there it is that he practices his hymns, perhaps writes them down, too, on moldy paper swollen with damp, out of the ferryman's garbled words I gathered that he, Jom, could be seen there, in his balled fist a stub of pencil, a flat, broad pencil thrown away by a carpenter, and the while he shook his head and spittle ran out of his mouth over his stubble of beard, he wrote and wrote but the rain washed it all right away. He, who is not capable of speech, makes these sounds come out, they sound like salve, malve, half, laugh, fold, cold, bold, rolled and so on, the words can be translated as you will. Still, now when I see him here I am not sure whether it really is he, rather I believe that the Jom the ferryman talks about sits today in one of the high-rise apartments in the suburbs, in an apartment with a high rental, at a writing table with a glass top, in front of a bare picture window looking out over playgrounds, auto factories and bus stops, and knows exactly where he is sitting and what he is writing down, and soberly he hammers out letter after letter, word after word on the typewriter and reads over the sentences, nodding his head.

Earlier at one time we went over this bridge, which sways under our feet. Its wood is rotten, it creaks at the joints, the pontoons are thickly crusted with bird droppings, the chains are overgrown with mussels and algae. There the traffic is held up, a horse has fallen in front of a coach, a roan sprinkled with red, the shafts are broken, the coachman stands by and curses, the occupants of the coach have gotten out, a bridal couple, her veil flutters, he holds his top hat, too large for him and hired for the occasion, fast on his head. Has a white chrysanthemum in his buttonhole and she carries a bunch of roses and the floor of the bridge sinks under the stalled traffic. Already the sirens and the policemen's whistles are coming and in the cars they sit patiently at the steering wheels, not yet knowing what has happened, will never know, only sit and wait in outpouring blue gas, wait and are everywhere awaited.

These windows, these tables, bookshelves and cabinets under the fluorescent lights, divided up by glass walls, when I look in on this place it seems to me I once went in and out here every day the year round, with great authority vested in me, the porter in his dark green uniform took off his cap to me on the stairs, people passing by bowed, a young lady in a tight jumper held the door open for me, stood ready with her stenographer's notebook when I walked into the room and sat down at the big desk. I laughed at myself, looking out from a richly decorated golden frame, broad-shouldered, rosy, with fillings in my teeth, and whoever else confronted me from the desk top, if not my wife and children, all were laughing and well-fed. No, a cloth hung over the picture on the wall, I could no longer bear to look at it, only during contract signings when the representatives of great organizations were present was the picture unveiled, and when my wife was announced, because she happened to be in town and needed money, for a hat, a tart, was her picture taken out of the drawer and placed on the desk top. I banished my assistant from the room, the hour had not yet come when I would go with her into the small side-room behind the padded door, where a couch stood ready and a table with drinks, it was early in the morning, I wanted to be alone and gird myself for the day. When she had shut the door behind her I threw myself down on the desk, put my head on my arms and sobbed for a quarter of an hour, then I straightened up in the swivel chair, the back of which could tip far back behind me, and thus sat, my hands locked behind my head, feet on the desk, and looked through the window out on the park, through which we are walking right now. Just as now the rocks were flying upward in great flocks, they were the forefathers of the present ones, the remote ancestors, and they scrawked hoarsely as their posterity scrawk today. On such a desk as the one on which my legs lay, in the morning the stack of incoming mail rises up, already taken out of the envelopes and spread out, and I read the heading of the topmost piece of writing, it comes from the Society for the Abolition of World Poverty. This must be an important office, a headquarters in which decisions of great moment are made. By all appearances it had to do with the distribution, lending or collection of money, I can no longer recall exactly, only remember the big figures that were discussed. Still shaken from time to time I leafed through the letters, underscored the sums named and drew little men on a sheet of paper that lay there ready for that purpose. Then I turned a knob on the intercom apparatus on my desk and right off breathing sounds could be heard coming from it, I needed only to whisper and a voice answered, and immediately thereafter she walked in, in her tight jumper, and the day's work could begin. Although both calculations and correspondence had been finished, the real activity consisted of seeking out, discarding and building up mutual relationships, in all the divisions, all this was hard to take in at a glance, seldom was obvious, for the most part lay concealed in operations that had a practical appearance, thus I could walk in anywhere and all I would see by a typewriter were two heads behind large unfolded papers, whereas down below out of sight hands held each other, or I saw the gaze of a person who carefully and regularly kept accounts apparently directed at a table of figures that he was holding up for me to see, whereas actually it was directed at a neck some distance away. Discussions of portfolios meant making rendezvous for the following evening, a hurried wandering together down the corridor had for its purpose not the completion of a series of telegrams but vanishing into a cloakroom. In my padded dictation room few words were lost, hardly was the door closed than she was pulling her jumper over her head and unbuttoning her dress and, after some days or weeks, according to the duration of our mutual accommodation, she carried out the same act of submission in other departments while new assistants made their appearance with me. And meanwhile our comprehensive effort flourished, it bloomed as money came pouring in, and what flowed out was expected as a matter of course to produce a multiple return, we had time for everything while the apparatus was working for us, and from the office boys' waiting room to the marble hall used by management's highest echelon we could all go our secret ways. No, I moved about in these rooms amid unspeakable toil, I walked sideways, my arms full of documents, carried them back and forth from one table to another, punched endless columns of figures into the machines, delivered reports, ran along the corridor to get new assignments, until I got a responsible post with the highest administrator, and for him took care of the purchase of wine-cellars, autos and racehorses, and was helpful to him in negotiations for a medieval fortress, with towers and moats. I had got used to walking sideways and dragged one leg behind me, and many here walked the same way, sideways or backward or bent far forward or taking a hop every third step, according to the kind of task with which they had been charged. If I am not mistaken in many of the rooms the secretaries were bound fast to their chairs, and when they stood up they carried their three-legged stools about with them on their behinds. When I think back on this time I see us all taking part in a tireless common effort, walking bent over, crawling, lying on our bellies between mechanical constructions, and only in the afternoon, in the hour between two and three, did we often sink into breathlessness, into a paralysis out of which only the scrawking of the rooks awakened us. No, it was not like that, I am seeing it wrong, it is so long ago, rather we found ourselves in an adventure, in a hectic game, in a raging tension, mornings we stormed up the stairs, threw ourselves at the mountain of incoming letters and telegrams, ripped the strips of paper out of the teletype which had ticked on throughout the night, and while we got the announcements and offers straightened out, with glowing zeal the loudspeaker system, the phones, the incoming messengers called to us to carry out new commissions, we had to come to our decisions lightning fast and function according to altered circumstance, we were breathless at our work in our main office, green eyeshades over our foreheads, black glasses before our eyes, gliding this way and that in the blinding light, numbers flashing all about us. Coffee, sandwiches were brought in, we had no time to go out to eat, and absence of a few minutes could destroy the work of years, could mean our ruin, until late at night we stuck it out and loaded mounting wealth into the safe. No, it was not like that, either, it was only a great disjointedness, a boundless agitation, in which we all kept watch on one another. I still see myself jumping up on a table, a heap of papers in my arms, and throwing the papers into the air, some of them folded into swallows, others into darts, others crumpled together, paper after paper, and then letter-files out of hard, pressed cardboard with a hole to hold them by the forefinger, they flew crosswise through the hall, some broke apart as they flew, and the leaves came tossing down, piled on top of each other, onto the typewriters and the buckled-down typists, and in a couple of places the glass partitions were smashed, faces appeared in the jagged holes, redly swollen, one running blood, and the typists leaped up with their chairs on their behinds and I jumped from desk to desk, sprang over the screaming typists and out of adjacent rooms the department heads, the assistant and general managers came running and a bunch from the board of directors and honorary chairmen, some of them were pushed in in wheelchairs, a meeting of the principal stockholders had just been held, and an old lady was flailing around with her umbrella, she was said to be the biggest investor, half of all profits belonged to her, her head trembled, she was carried by two general directors and right away one of the portfolios hit her, slung sure of its aim, backward she fell, her legs, in black woolen stockings, kicked about in her petticoats and outside the rooks threw themselves at the windowpanes, dashed with yellow beaks against the vibrating glass. Oh no, I sat patiently and unobtrusively at my desk, wearing black protective sleevelets in order to preserve the jacket of my only suit, mornings I came to my duties punctually, and evenings I rode back in a bus, a firmly wedged-in part of the whole, arm in arm, shoulder to shoulder with my own kinds, in the flow of the street.

Here, behind the freight depot, at this spot between high factory buildings, one time I was lying behind the boxwood bushes in the enclosure at the train platform fence. I had landed here after being unable to solve certain problems in connection with wife and child. I don't know how long I tried to find a solution, whether I assumed from the start that finding a solution was out of the question and only pretended it might be possible. In any case I had been preoccupied with the matter for a long time, the child had already learned to talk when I took off this evening. My attempt to solve the problem, or at least my alleged attempt, was involved in almost everything that went on in the apartment. I picked up a plate, my wife asked, why that particular plate. I explained, while holding up the plate between thumb and forefinger, that the plate seemed to be suitable for the purpose I had in mind. For what purpose, she inquired. My answer was, for example, for the purpose of holding the food I had it in mind to cook. What kind of food, my wife asked. Noodles, for instance. Or grits, or beans. To her the plate seemed too small for that. Or, if baked cheese slices, or plum dumplings were in prospect, too large, there was no need to fill it full. She considered this to be superfluous and brought to my attention the fact that the very multiplicity of plates which she had brought as a dowry was to make it possible to have the proper plate at any given time. In a united effort we selected other plates from among the high piles of porcelain with which the cupboard was filled, in the course of which maneuver towers of plates were taken down and had to be put back again one on top of the other, always making sure that the child did not run into the unloaded heaps. I said to my wife, stick to your machine, do your work, I'll do mine, but she said that even I could see how far I was getting with my work. If I said it's better that you finish sewing the nightgowns that have been ordered and leave setting the table to me, she said how much it meant to her that this time we ate from the plates with the checkered blue pattern at the rim and that anyhow she had to sew shirts and blouses far into the night. Also in the cupboard were our towels, tablecloths and sheets, and, since they partly covered the tableware, had to be taken out of the drawers and, since they would get dirty on the floor, laid out on the bed. I took out a glass. The glasses were packed closely together in the topmost drawer, and in order to choose among them I had to climb up on a chair. We had numerous kinds of glasses, all in all the contents of the cupboard constituted our sole riches, everything else hardly bore mentioning. When I had taken out a glass for myself, a glass for my wife and a third glass suited for the child and had put the glasses on the table, she asked why I had picked out those glasses. I explained to her that in my opinion the form and volumetric capacity of the glasses in question were in line with the drinks that I intended to pour into them for the meal. For example, water, or beer. These glasses, she retorted, were intended for wine. And so again we climbed up, I meanwhile drawing up a second chair, up to the cupboard. Again I placed the glasses I had removed back in the drawer and instead took out the glasses that my wife preferred, while the child crept under the chairs and had his hand trodden on by me stepping down. Taking care of the hand led to numerous differences of opinion. I wanted to wash the hand, my wife found washing injurious in this case. I came up with a band-aid, my wife found that in this case a bandage was better. I bound the hand with the bandage, but it had to be un-bound, because I had wound it too tight. Meanwhile the dish that I had in the pot or pan had boiled away or burned up, it was always hard for me to keep to the pre-cise boiling or broiling time, and my wife asked me whether she had to do all the boiling and broiling, too. At this point the discussions were already becoming more involved and could not be settled by a simple for or against, in which my wife's viewpoint finally won the day. I had taken over the cooking, table-setting, dishwashing, clean-ing up and childcaring, since my wife was supporting us with her work on the sewing machine. When now and then there was a quarter of an hour during which the child had fallen asleep and no pressing chore lay at hand, I devoted myself to another activity, I sat down at the table, that is, if the table were clear, and not filled with pieces of clothing that had to be sewed, and spread my papers out in front of me, the papers on which I had written the notes for my scientific work. I tried to read what I had written down and to remember what it was I wanted to say with the matter inscribed. Scarcely was I sitting still, bent over the papers, face propped on my hand, forehead wrinkled, than my wife turned to me. She had a thread in her mouth and her feet kept right on working at the treadle under the machine, she nodded at me and asked how I was getting along. I could not miss hearing a note of contempt in her query and I replied, if I had the peace of mind and the leisure, and she nodded again and said, the thread be-tween her lips, that in such case we would have the peace of mind and leisure to starve. Since she was right I could say nothing to this and the quarter-hour passed without my

grasping the sense of the notes, let alone writing down anything new. Finally I just sat there, leaned back, had a look
at the ceiling and walls of the room, our bed, the child's
crib, my wife's back, the pieces of fabric hanging over
chairbacks, the round-breasted torso of the dressmaker's
dummy, the cupboard, that great lump of a portable cupboard, which took up a third of the room, the kitchen
nook, the door to the washroom, the door to the corridor,
the window beyond which all to be seen was a building
front with other windows. When I wasn't writing I still
had to take care of my pipe, I knocked out the ashes, dug
the oily tobacco dottle out of the bowl, twisted off the
stem, cleaned the nicotine residue out of it, shoved the
pipe together again, filled it, lighted it up, let the smoke
come puffing out, while the sewing-machine needle fren-
ziedly pierced the cloth, my wife bent forward, bit off the
thread, turned the cloth to a new position and then, having
become suspicious because of the quiet at the table, turned
toward me, her feet always tramping away at the treadle.
She said I was getting everything dirty with my ashes and
tobacco leavings. I replied that the by-products of my
smoking were going into an ashtray. She said that my
smoking was hurting the child. Complicated trains of
thought lay behind her criticism, for she meant not only
the smoking, in the smoking she saw only an expression
of my idleness, and I tried to explain to her that smoking
stimulated my brain, that while I was sitting still I was full
of meditation. Yet when she bent at this to her work once
more with a snuffing sound from her nose, I had to admit
she was right, for the pipe-smoking did not in fact lead to
any world-shaking results, all that happened was that I
heard the spittle bubbling in the tobacco, my throat hurt
from the biting smoke and the ashes, the burnt matches and
the sooty, gummy tobacco dottle merely represented so
much money thrown away, and I strove to find one small

detail in the complicated process that stood in my favor, yet none did I find. I knew before I started that when I sat down at the table I would accomplish nothing in the short span of time allotted me, and yet sit down I did, took out my papers, looked up some inconsequential thing or other. Even when on one occasion I wrote something down on the paper I knew that it said nothing, nonetheless I wrote it down, read it over, nodded and pretended that it meant something to me. For some minutes I threw up a bulwark, I entrenched myself behind the papers, and the pencil was my weapon. The pencil point broke, it had to be sharpened. That took some time. The knife was full and had to be whetted. The pencil-dust and the shavings had to be cleared away. And then the child woke up, or I had to run to the market because I had forgotten the onions for the herring. In the evening when the child had grown quiet with the aid of a soporific, when the plates had been washed up and put back into the closet, the pots scoured, the table wiped clean, the day's expenditures totted up, I might perhaps have had more time for my writing activity, but it was just now that most of the customers came, fetched finished sewing jobs, brought new ones, haggled about the price, tried on blouses, skirts, jackets a number of times, during which business I had to withdraw into the bathroom. Sitting on the toilet I had my best thoughts, thoughts which in any event for a while seemed meaningful to me, but when I went into them more closely they, too, proved to be no good. Later in the evening when the last customers had gone, my wife naturally was tired, I myself was not tired, however much taking care of the house took up my time. I wanted to sit some more in my chair, but my wife wanted to sleep and the light burning prevented her from doing it. When she took her clothes off I wanted to take hold of her, when I saw her in her slip, or naked, I lusted for her, yet she said, what do you want, what are you grabbing me for. I stroked her flat breasts and thin hips, yet when I pulled her into the bed I had to turn the light out, she wanted to lie in the dark. It took quite a while for my eyes to get used to the subdued shimmer of light that came through the window from the streetlamps. It was hard to tell whether my wife was asleep or awake, she had closed her eyes, did not move, let out not a sound, while I was busy with her. Gradually the objects in the room became distinct, the dressmaker's dummy with its little round head, its broad hips, its erect bosom stood at the foot of the bed and watched my exertions. I got up, took the dummy under the arm and hid her behind the cupboard. It was on such a night, when the collective laughter of a quiz-hodgepodge and the rush of waterfalls was penetrating through the walls that I suddenly sprang out of bed, dressed and ran out, landed in freight-station precincts and there threw myself down behind the box-wood hedge. Years later I learned what she had kept from me. In her eyes I was a criminal, I behaved like a madman in her apartment, hit her, threw silverware at her head, and when her customers had undressed I came leaping out of the toilet where she had sequestered me, so they had to flee screaming into the hall, and while the child howled I threw myself on her, tore off her clothes, tipped over the sewing machine and finally flung myself headfirst out through the window, unfortunately not smashing myself to smithereens in the street.

The ferryman told me once about his wife. He described her differently to me than I remembered her. I saw her as still fleshy, stout, with her hair drawn back in a bun on her neck, with a wart on her nose and I did not recognize the picture he had of her, for he described her as haggard, almost a head taller than he, with red hair, apparently a wig, and he knew nothing about a wart on her nose, on the contrary, he told about a growth of beard unknown to me. He told me how evenings she sat before the door of the house and sang. Without taking his pipe out of his mouth he imitated the tone of this singing, it was like a yowling or the bleating of sheep, and this seemed to be true to the mark, for according to what he said the animals whose voices she was mimicking when she sang slowly came to her from all sides and listened to her, and yowled, meowed and bleated along with her, and while she sang she kept her eyes closed and swayed from side to side. The ferryman, too, went outdoors when this singing was going on, and one or the other of the sons, above all Jom, the oldest, who here learned the rudiments of his later litanies, and because she sang only on beautiful evenings, and not when it was stormy or raining, a yellowish or greenish sky was to be seen, and beyond the river lay the city, with the windows in the houses yellowish or greenish. In winter, when snow lay deep about the house and the animals were in the barn and it was inadvisable on account of the weather to go outdoors, sometimes the wife went into a dance, by the full of the moon, I believe. The ferryman showed me, standing at the steering wheel, his idea of this dance, alternately he raised the right then the left leg to one side, letting the other fall, and I saw that he had tears in his eyes. For now the other wife came to his mind, the other wife into which one day this one had turned. She went to put food for Jym in front of the box, as she did every evening, she went out with the full wooden trough and came in without a trough, as usual, yet now she was small and shriveled, a little dwarf, sharp-nosed, crook-legged, with stringy black hair, red eyes. Who are you. I'm your wife, she said. Weren't you just tall and red-haired. No, I am as I am, am as I am, she replied. She stayed that way. She danced no more and she sang no more, yet other than that she did all her work as before, only more slowly, more helplessly.

That time on the island, during the night I was telling you about, for the first time I saw what leaves are. When I had gone up to the house and was standing in front of the bushes and trees I saw those thousands of leaves, each in a different place fastened to the branch with a thin stalk, and each leaf moved, rose and fell, quivered this way and that, still silvery bright on the surface, darkly shadowed below, and in the rising wind the branches lifted, became pressed downward, in a common rhythm, and the thousands of leaves struck each other softly, thousands of thin, rattling little plates, each shot through with veins, with a fine venation running from the middle vein outward, each arranged according to the same system, and yet each different from the other, still the flickering light lay on them, and in their twistings and turnings they reflected the lightness that broke through the tattered cloud, and then the trunks began to bend and straighten up again, and when they went down the leaves, standing upright on their stems, rushed downward, and when the trunks rose the leaves rose, bent backward, with a whistling sound, and this repeated itself constantly, while the clouds massed ever more thickly together and shut off the light. For a long time I stood in front of the house under the spell of the rushing sound, of the dance of the trees, and as I stood there it was as if I were stretching myself out, away over the hill and as far as into the woods, my fear lay spread about in the grasses, the woodland, the cliffs, was taken up by all the leaves, and stormed back on me again, with the surf-foam, the buffets of the storm.

What I said about the ferryman's former house was wrong.
I have never been in the house, I have only stood at the
fence and thought I could see the kitchen through the
window, with the whitewashed superstructure of the fireplace, I looked between the fence pickets, between the
sorrel leaves, and saw how the woman came with the pails
from milking. In the barn the calves lowed and the cows
called back from the field, there was a lamentation in this
calling out, for the calves were not allowed to be with
their mothers, they stood held fast by wooden stanchions,
immediately after birth they were taken from their mothers,
they cried for their mothers' teats and the cows cried out
for their young ones' soft muzzles, but only the pummeling
hands of the ferryman's wife pulled at their udders, drawing the fat foaming milk out of them into the pail, and the
calves got a watery mixture poured into the trough, and
over this they yammered and the cows lifted their heads
and stared with big uncomprehending eyes out over the
city, and let out their own muffled cries. When the ferryman's house was torn down and the excavations began for
the new buildings, Jum, the fat one, was left behind on
the old property. It is said that he did not want to leave
the place of his birth, that no power was great enough to
drive him out of bed and out into all the world's winds.
In his description of the collapse of the household the
ferryman did not mention his wife and the other sons, it is
possible at the time he was living alone with his favorite
son. Long ago the surveyors had come with their white
stakes and had rammed them into the ground, the fence
had been knocked down by tractors with caterpillar treads,
there were no more cattle nor any barn and the trees lay
there with their roots become all cartilaginous. The frame
of the building was already going up and the brightly
painted kettle of the cement-mixer turned. Ladders were
laid against the leany old house, workmen climbed up them,

whistling and singing, and lifted the tiles from the roof and, using rammers, hit the walls from the inside so that beams and stones fell in heaps. In the clouds of dust Jum lay there in bed, the eiderdown coverlet drawn up over his ears and in between the trips he had to make down below on the river the ferryman ran up to him, sat by him, held his hand, fed him and talked baby-talk to him. The crumbled stones were carted away and when the floor planking was loosened workmen lifted the bed and put it to one side on a wall of earth. It was to be seen standing there for a long time, amid the building framework, the cranes, the piles of lumber and tar pots, soon it was overlaid by a thick layer of dust and mortar, which the ferryman brushed away every night as best he could. The ferryman's new shack was already standing down on the riverbank, yet he spent the night up above out in the open next to his son's sleeping-place, leaned on the edge of the bed, his legs drawn up to his body. The high buildings grew, the bed with the recumbent one on it was shoved here and there, and often it was banged or run into hard, the legs were broken off, only the mattress still held together, and there lay Jum wrapped in his blanket, and could look up at the windows of the telegraph office, out of which the lady telegraphists, just moved in, threw him kisses. For they, too, soon loved him, they loved the shining full moon of his face and his round belly showing itself under the blanket, and during their coffee breaks they brought him coffee and cakes. And the impression arose, according to the ferryman's description, that the bed is still there, among the big buildings, perhaps behind the service-truck garage, on the courtyard level, from which point the cupola skylight windows rise up at regular intervals.

I lived in this house on the fifth story at the time the office

in the top story was being set up. Mostly I lay in bed,
stretched out flat on my back, and only occasionally went
to the broad window, to the table with the glass top, and
looked out onto the playgrounds, repair shops and bus
stops. Mornings, half-awake, I often saw a field in my
mind's eye before me, brightly lit by the sun, I saw every
blade of grass, with clover, poppies, cuckoo-flowers among
it, the smell was there and I scented it in the wind, I held
fast to this image, slowly I soared along with it, until other
images came, there I was lying under boards and pulpy
cardboard at the edge of the river, in front of the railroad
bridge, and saw the nightly manifestations and the manifestations of the daytime, and whatever showed itself was
unclear and only illusion, and the only actuality was a hand,
or a foot, and this limb thrust itself through the thin wall
that surrounded me and forced its way in, and it was
covered with stiff hairs, it was part of no body, it was an
independent organism, it crept up to me in a place where
the air was sticky and viscid, and then I saw that already
this space was filled with masses of the same kind of moving
things, big feet, hands, rumps and necks, all covered with
hair and scurfy, many with mouths mutely opening and
closing, there were also rows of teeth with tatters of flesh
on them, and half-ears in the bloody encrustations of which
gold glittered, and fingers with jewels embedded right in
them, and all this moved under me, and it was up to me to
find out what kind of puddle, pit this was, and sometimes
I got as far as my pile of boards, for long intervals felt
safely hidden in my lair, or I pushed my way even as far
as my bed, on which I lay flat, capable of no other movement except to bore into my nose, than to twist my head
to one side and cast a look outside at the new buildings,
then the other thing was there again and this time it began
with a sucking, my mouth still sucked itself tightly shut
and then was torn away, or that on which it had been

sucking was torn away, spittle ran out of my mouth, and there were lips to be seen, strained wide open, with wet teeth inside and a tongue stretched out that made twisting movements, yet out of this mouth blood was already gushing and the bleeding mouth crept back over small heads of cabbage thickly planted together, over burst skulls, set in rows in a field, and they all snapped with little mouths and opened and closed little eyes, and each face was formed in its own special way, with special skin blemishes, summer freckles, with a scar, a dimple, a pair of steel specs. I made a superhuman effort to explain all this to myself, and doing it thought about a white sheet of paper the emptiness of which could be completely filled up with words, and I heard myself babble, babble all a-dabble scrabble gabble rabble fabble, dame came name lame fame same, taste paste haste waste, hand sand land, sing spring, wind sinned, think stink sink dink wink pink rinkydinky finky, donkey tonky, piss hiss niche witch bitch ditch turn spurn earn learn see pee mow go hickerydickery slithermithery hoppetyho, but these or similar words eluded me, covered nothing up at all, I could only make this lalling and babbling, it was all taken up, this mass of words, by one perception, yet this perception was only that I understood nothing, could explain nothing, and all that I wanted was to simplify my situation, well then, I thought, I have run away from my wife and my children have been dashed against the wall, they have probably flung me into a jail and then, as they usually do, into a mass grave, and now I must bear witness, give reckoning, for a life with all its ways run and left behind, all doors opened and closed, all its movements and its touchings, its words, that flood of words uttered and taken in, to no other end than to have them trickle away, melt into a blur, come to nothing. And there I lay, among the fragmentations creeping all about, amid this overflowing mass of limbs all soundlessly opening and closing their mouths, and each mouth was a bloodied hole, and over it all grew hair, and nails sprouted on the wandering fingers and toes, and far above us, on hard-trampled ground which had been replanted with grass and shrubs, that was where the sounds came from, and when I strove even more I could hear how up above it was cracking and crunching and how at the same time there was a singing and whistling, and then I burrowed my way upward, although that is really impossible, and got to a point somewhere in front of this field, these grasses, this wind, lay a long time under piles of boards, until in the spring the snow melted and the ground opened up in many places in small, perfectly round craters, and out of each an arm stuck up, a foot, a head with an open mouth, and it was hair that was waving among the grasses. Thus I lay, as the attic story over me was renovated, sucked on my fingers, turned my head toward the window, imagined myself a meadow in the wind and also became active again, too, and bestirred myself, despite my supposed fatigue, to get up and out. An ordinary morning, with the sounds of people working. I woke up to a brief burst of ringing on the phone. When I took the receiver off the hook nothing but a scratching and a crackling were to be heard, then the connection went dead. I put on my bathrobe and went to the apartment door in slippers, my pajama pants, which were too big for me, and which I held together about my body. In the stairwell painters were standing on ladders and with jets of flame from their blowtorches were scorching paint off the walls, the layers of paint bubbled and boiled, blew up into fat blisters and curled in brown flaps about the scraping putty-knives. The flames had strayed over the wires which hung bare on the wall and which led to a junction box over my door, I pointed up at them with my finger and said they had been burnt out, and what I said was not intelligible in the harsh sizzling. I climbed a couple of rungs up a ladder and screamed my complaint into the roaring and was told that I would have to talk to the foreman. Holding to my pants tight I went down between the scaffolding and the heaps of charred paint-bark, down the stairs to the newly built rooms in which employees were already putting papers and volumes of documents into cabinets and onto shelves, and carrying chairs, desks, type-writers and adding machines here and there. I called for the foreman and the cry echoed strangely in my own ears. In the corridor a linoleum runner was being stretched out and fastened down, I had to jump over the roll as it came my way and doing so lost a slipper. I bent down to look for the slipper, but could not find it among the cardboard boxes filled with printed matter and clerical equipment, was also hampered by the pajama pants which kept slipping down. I asked a couple of secretaries who were carrying a swivel-chair by me where the foreman was, and they only looked at me with eyebrows raised. I rubbed the sleep out of my eyes and went on, one foot slippered the other naked, and came into a room in which men in white smocks were standing at a table looking down over blueprints spread out. I asked them for the foreman, they turned to me and looked me over, and when I explained to them that my phone wires in the stairwell had been destroyed, all that they said, while looking at my naked foot and the hand I kept under the bathrobe to hold up my pants, was that it had nothing to do with them. I made it known to them that I had suffered a substantial loss through the loss of my phone connection, that I did most of my business over the phone. I lived from selling books, was an agent for horticul-tural publications, expensive works on the art of cookery, horticulture and infant care, and during the forenoon hours carried on conversations with people who, the evening before, I had carefully selected from the phone book according to a certain system, and told them how good the books were and how attractive the purchase terms. After this explanation the building bosses directed me to a phone company man who was supposed to be busy somewhere in the entrance hall. Two employees carrying in a green fireproof strongbox pushed me to one side, and I again went out into the corridor to look for the phone company man. I called out for him and again became aware of the strange sound of my voice and then I spied him behind a glass partition, installing a switchboard. He turned his face up to me, his forehead was wrinkled, and between his lips he held a series of screws and plugs. He directed me to the main office and got busy again with the varicolored phone cable wires that had been separated and stuck up in bundles out of the switchboard. I turned about and went back down the corridor, where once again I rummaged among the boxes and office furniture in search of my lost slipper. An older woman, possibly a bookkeeper or cashier, asked me what I was looking for. I replied that while in search of someone whom I could make responsible for the damage done to my phone connection, my slipper, as I was jumping over the roll of linoleum runner, had fallen from my foot, and she promised, in a soothing tone, that soon new phone services would be installed, and my slipper, if it was found, would be returned to me, something that brought tears to my eyes, and so I went back to my room, where I took the path of least resistance and waited for the day to pass.

And once we were riding in a coach, drawn by a runaway horse, the reins were broken, the coachman had fallen off the seat, round the square stormed the horse until in front of the hotel in which the room was all ready and waiting for us the porter and houseman, as well as a couple of policemen who had come hurrying up, grabbed hold of the harness straps and brought the horse to a standstill.

While the redly speckled horse was rearing up and snuffing and throwing his head back, the big door was held open ahead of us, we walked up on red carpeting, the door to the room was opened and then shut again behind us, at the sides of the open balcony window the drapes fluttered, and outside lay the city, oh this city, which we had never seen, those buildings in yellow ochre, those green roofs, that sky of inimitable blue. Similarly, now, we had ridden through a snowstorm, and now warmth streamed toward us, dry sandy salty warmth. And although we had spent a year, perhaps seven years, with one another, it was as if we were touching each other for the first time. After a long separation, a long separation we stripped off each other's clothes from our skin, and our eyes were wide open so as to see each other's every movement, and her face was white, white as the walls of the room, and her teeth glittered as if she were laughing about something inconceivably amazing, and so we breathed on one another, and from outdoors this light came piercing in, a light that we knew from no dream. Oh, this changed city, these hours of re-union after forgotten days and nights, these hours until dawn when she had become so attenuated that I hardly saw her any more, only felt her, on my knees, her face could still be faintly seen, her arms lay about my neck, yet she was lifeless, or sunken into deep sleep, only once did her eyelids move slightly, they lifted just a crack only to close again, and when the cock crowed on the balcony under our window she had vanished, it had become light, it had become blindingly light, she had vanished, yet I still felt her, in the flat of my hand, and there, too, where my other hand was missing I felt her, her skin, her hair, yet the city outside already again was as it always was, as it always was.

The house into which my father went, this big white house

117 ✒

with many windows, its walls covered with slabs of white stone, I do not know how I should describe this house, whether it should be called beautiful or ugly, or whether within it could be lived in at all. Every single piece of stone facing is screwed fast into the wall decoration at the four corners, the stone is shot through with bluish veins, there is copper flashing at each window frame. This facade is there to show wealth, many stones, many windows, so many that I cannot count them, and yet at one time they were nevertheless counted. Marble and copper, on and on we walk past this facade, along past these countless windows, these countless white slabs of stone. There he comes again out of the big front door, he is walking stiff and straight, hands in the pockets of his topcoat and the heels of his shoes click in regular beat on the sidewalk. Perhaps he is taking a walk after the day's work, he is going the rounds of his property, enjoying the evening air, looking up proudly at the gigantic white block, at this factory, this world-girdling business house, this work of a lifetime, he breathes in deeply, he is still in full possession of his powers, comes back in again through the entrance, rides upstairs on the chair-elevator, sticks the key from the bunch of keys into the keyhole of the door, turns the key, presses down the latch, goes into the hallway, making noises which always make an impression on his children in the depths of the apartment. Yet it seems to me his topcoat is shabby and the heels of his shoes worn down. Perhaps he is only the doorkeeper here. His shoulders are weary, his head is sunken down, he takes his hands out of his pockets and they dangle limply at his sides. Yes, my father was always worried, was always ready to be put upon and upbraided, he had never made it beyond night porter, for days on end he probably had never dared ask house visitors what it might be they wanted, timidly he walked across the courtyard, perhaps to take care of the furnace, or unloaded the firewood, and only at night could he sit at the window of his cubby at the entrance-way, behind double-barred gratings. We lived in lodgings, in a couple of small rooms, and certainly it was not in this house, but in another smaller older one. Nights from my bed, through the glass door, in the panes of which a couple of bent tulip stems were cut, I could see my father on the chair near his dormer window, hours on end I saw his face, which he kept tensely turned toward the gate and his hand lay ready on the alarm-bell button, yet never, never did he press the button and the bell did not sound, and my brothers lay in their beds and slept, and in the adjoining room my mother snored. I know how every night I struggled against the impulse to go out there to him, who sat there so mutely, and once I did it perhaps, for it seems to me as if I can remember seeing how his face crinkled into a smile, and how for a moment he took his hand from the bell button and stroked me on my forehead. This moment often comes back to me, at night in some street or other, or when I am going down the stairs in some house or other then it is as if I were going downstairs here, and right away I am off into nowhere, a great span of time behind me and before me a great span of time, and at this moment just a couple of steps in a street or on some stairs or other and presto I have vanished into this other world.

And now I see the ferryman's house, as it looked at that time, when I had climbed up one evening from the riverbank. It was a small house, made of planks painted dark red and with white corner-posts and blue window frames. The ferryman had come up after the day's work, he had closed the garden gate behind him and had gone along the path to the door of the house. From the field where a couple of cows were grazing came a woman with a milk pail, she was a thin, dark-haired woman with a knot of black hair at the nape of her neck. She went into the house without looking to right or left, and yet he was standing only a couple of steps away from her. He took the small stubby pipe he had been smoking out of his mouth, knocked it out on the stone steps in front of the door and stuck it in his pocket. He stood for a long time at the door and solitary sounds came up from the city and a cow mooed from the meadow. Then he went into the house, and for a long time nothing happened, I sat at the edge of the road and nobody came by, and in the house it was quiet and a bird with long red tail-feathers flew over and from far away came some sort of bang. Suddenly the woman ran out of the door with her skirt flying and her hair waving loose behind her, she ran to the barn with big bounds unhindered by her heavy shoes and the ferryman came rushing out of the door behind her, his knee buckled as he hit the ground, yet he got up and flew after her and both disappeared into the barn. Again it was still for a long time, I ducked down low in the leafiness at the fence and held my breath, and then I saw a gigantic figure emerge from the house, a man with a naked hairy torso and long reddish brown hair on his head braided into braids at the side, with a wildly growing beard, with tremendously knotty arms, the skin of them overrun with tattoos, wearing boots that reached over his knees and which had the tops turned down and spurs at the heels. He opened his mouth wide and in the dark cavern single yellow teeth could be seen, he pumped his chest full of air, and I waited for his outcry, yet everything stayed still, he just stood there, with his powerful gaping, and slowly turned round and went back into the house. And I crept down the road and ran breathlessly along the path on the riverbank, here, where streets have now been built, bridges and under-pinnings for wharves, here where we are walking now, where we are walking walking walking